TWO-GUN HERO

WALT SLADE, undercover ace of the Texas Rangers, has the slowest temper and the fastest guns in the southwest. Tall, soft-spoken, and dedicated to law, Slade volunteers for the most dangerous missions in Texas—a land beyond the law. Owlhoots fear the sight of this lone lawman, gunslingers out to get a reputation dare him to gunplay—from which there is no return. Many times Slade has stood in the shadow of death, but never has he been marked for cold-blooded murder as in **GUNDOWN!**, a tense story of border rivalry.

TWO-FISTED AUTHOR

BRADFORD SCOTT, a rugged keen-eyed westerner with the vitality of the wide-open spaces, has lived close to death all of his life. He fought in the Mexican Revolution, sailed around Cape Horn, and served in the French Foreign Legion. His later career as a bridge builder and mining engineer has given him the detailed knowledge of western country which has allowed him to write **GUNDOWN!** and other top-notch novels of the west.

GUNDOWN!

BRADFORD SCOTT

WILDSIDE PRESS

First printing, February 1963

ONE

RANGER WALT SLADE, whom the Mexicans of the Rio Grande River villages named *El Halcón*—The Hawk—rode into the cowtown of Olton looking like the frazzled end of a misspent life. His boots were scuffed and scratched, with a couple of holes in them, the result of stumbling against sharp flints. His Levi's—bibless overalls—and his faded-blue shirt were stained and streaked with dust and boasted a few rents that came from blundering into the straggle of a mesquite thicket in the black dark. Even his broad-brimmed "J.B." had a discouraged look and was also stained and streaked. And there was a tear in the brim that was *not* made by a mesquite thorn. His gray eyes were red-rimmed and bloodshot. A four days' growth of beard that was black as his hair stubbled his lean cheeks.

Not that there was anything remarkable about his unkempt appearance. One does not ride across fifty miles of alkali desert in a raging storm without acquiring a few wear and tear mementos. Especially when one walks a good part of the time to keep the icy wind and equally icy rain from turning one's blood into ice cream.

About the only thing presentable were his heavy black guns snugged in their carefully worked and oiled cut-out holsters. Nothing had a deleterious effect on those big Colt forty-fives.

His well worn but excellent riding gear had also suffered quite a bit. A little oil and rubbing would take care of that, however. And even Shadow, his magnificent black horse, was hardly up to snuff. His usually satiny coat was smudged and rumpled, and he hung his head dejectedly from sheer weariness.

His master also was deadly tired and darned hungry. His normally keen vision was slightly blurred, and his eyelids twitched.

But despite his lack of physical well being, Slade glanced

5

about with quickening interest as he rode through the outskirts of the town. The lovely blue dusk of a day that had ended up fine was sifting down from the surrounding hills like an impalpable mist. The eastern crags were bathed in a soft glow and the rugged battlements to the west were ringed about with saffron flame.

Windows were changing from darkly staring eyes to squares and rectangles of ruddy gold. Atop poles, lanterns that served as street lights began to wink, as an old Mexican with a tall ladder touched flame to the wicks. The board sidewalks of the main street resounded to the clump of boots that provided an undertone to the whirl and patter of words, the bawling of song, and the whine of fiddles that drifted over the swinging doors of saloon, dance hall and gambling hall. Slade saw many cowboys in careless but efficient attire, gaudy handkerchiefs looped about their sinewy throats, guns swinging low against their thighs. There was a sprinkling of Mexicans, some in tatters and bare of foot, unkempt hair topped by enormous steeple-crowned sombreros encrusted with silver. Others were darkly picturesque in short jackets and tight pantaloons of black velvet likewise adorned with silver conchas. For this was a Border town with *Méjico* not far away. Riders clicked along, their horses' irons kicking up little puffs of dust from the already drying street. There was a smell of sweat, horse flesh, and the singed hair of cattle.

To the south, curving around the town, and flanked by an arid, seemingly illimitable expanse of desert—the desert Slade had crossed—gleamed the twin ribbons of steel of a railroad. Even as Slade gazed, a train roared westward without pausing, leaving behind its swirl of smoke and the pungent tang of hot oil, sulphur and creosote. Following the line of the railroad with his eye, Slade noted extensive loading pens and a number of sidings. The town evidently rated importance as a cattle shipping point, the kind of town that sometimes mushrooms from a railroad building camp. Which was so in this instance. The wide, hill-surrounded valley to the north and east, grown with wheat and needle grass and apparently well watered, hinted at big herds.

"Nice looking country, all right," Slade remarked to Shadow, "a prosperous appearing pueblo. Horse, I've a hunch this is it. The hellions wouldn't have much farther they could go, unless they kept on and slid across into Mexico, which

I don't believe they did. Not much worth while for them over there, and I've a notion this section would provide fat pickings for an enterprising owlhoot bunch. From what Captain Jim said, they've sure been cutting a swath across half of Texas. Yes, I've a notion they'll squat for a while somewhere hereabouts. Well, we'll see. Now for a stable where you can put on the nosebag and get cleaned up."

Shadow raised his head and snorted cheerful agreement. He appeared in good conditon, aside from being a bit mussed up, despite the fact he had covered several hundred miles in the past week, including his terrapin-brained master's mistake in taking a short cut across that infernal desert, which proved to be a darned "long" cut, what with the storm and everything else.

Glancing down a side street, Slade spotted a swinging sign that proclaimed. "Livry Stabel." He chuckled.

"Sort of simplified spelling, but I reckon this is it," he commented as he unforked.

Repeated hammering brought the stablekeeper to the door, a crusty looking old gent with bristling white whiskers and intolerant eyes. He glanced at Slade, gazed at Shadow.

"Hoppin' horned toads! What a cayuse!" he exclaimed. "Bring him in, bring him in." He stretched out a fearless hand.

"Careful," Slade warned. "Easy, Shadow!"

The big black's ears had flattened back on his head. In answer to Slade's voice they pricked forward again and he thrust his velvety muzzle into the gnarled hand and blew softly through his nose.

"You'll do," Slade said to the keeper. "Give him a big helping of oats, and if you have a brush and a currycomb handy, I'll clean him up a bit."

"Never mind, never mind," replied the keeper. "I'll take care of him. I like to take care of horses, especially prime ones like this one. Never saw a finer."

"He'll do," Slade said. "Thank you."

"Uh-huh, and he'll be here when you come for him; I got a Sharpe's buffalo gun and an itchy trigger finger that say so." He ran his eye over Slade's dusty form.

"Trough in the back and soap and a clean towel if you'd like to take a dip," he added gruffly. "Water's a mite cold but it runs fresh and it'll take the dust off."

7

"Thanks again," Slade answered. "I can sure use one about now."

The stablekeeper nodded. "Rode the chuck line in my time," he said. "Know a good wash perks a feller up a bit after he's been in the saddle for a spell."

Slade's lip twitched slightly. Not strange that the keeper mistook him for a range tramp—he was forced to admit he looked the part, all right, in his present condition. Which was exactly what he wanted to look like.

The water was cold, but after a good sluicing Slade felt considerably better. He fingered the stubble of the black beard and decided a shave could wait a while. Didn't feel up to it right now and besides it fitted well with the character he had assumed. For the same reason, he donned the disreputable garments he had shucked off instead of the spares in his pouches. He combed his thick black hair, batted his hat into some semblance of shape and returned to the keeper.

"A place to sleep?" that worthy replied to his question. "I got a vacant room over the stalls, alongside mine, if you like to sleep close to your horse, which I reckon you do. Clean, and no bugs. You can put your rig in there—door to the right at the head of the stairs. I'll give you a key to the front door. Don't often hand 'em out, but a feller who rides a horse like this one has to be okay. Try and not tear the place down when you come in drunk; I don't like to be woke up in the middle of the night. Place to eat? You might try Francia's, right around the corner. Chuck is good, and so are the drinks. Everything okay, if you can stomach Francia."

"I've no intention of making my dinner off Francia, whoever she or he is," Slade smiled. The keeper chuckled.

"Reckon you'd find her sorta hard to digest, but if you managed to get her down, there's one thing I'll say for her," he continued, "you'd have more brains in your belly than you've likely got in your head."

Slade laughed outright. The old keeper chuckled again and got busy with his currycomb.

"Guess I'll take a chance on Francia's place," Slade said and walked out. He was not particularly perturbed by the keeper's dubious recommendation. He'd contacted the Francia sort before—tough old harridans, but they almost always ran a first class place.

So he did not hesitate when he saw, done in red lettering on a wide window,

FRANCIA'S

He pushed through the swinging doors and looked around.

Although it was a little past sunset, the large room was already pretty well crowded. It boasted a long bar, two roulette wheels, a dance floor, a faro bank, poker tables, and also tables to accommodate diners who preferred more leisure and comfort than afforded by the stand-up lunch counter over to one side.

At the moment, all the dining tables were occupied. Slade desired a leisurely meal and seeing that a group at a far table appeared ready to leave before long, he approached the lunch counter in quest of something to take the sharp edge off his hunger while he waited.

A cheese sandwich caught his eye. Both cheese and bread looked fresh and inviting. He put down a dime, received the sandwich and went to work on it, glancing at the still occupied table from time to time. He had finished it to the last crumb and was still chewing slowly when a voice spoke behind him, "I've a notion you could eat more than that, cowboy."

The voice was a woman's voice and Slade turned, and stared.

"What in blazes!" fleeted through his mind. "A fugitive from the *Pirates of Penzance?*"

TWO

THE WOMAN WHO SPOKE—girl, rather, for she was not more than twenty-two or three at the most—would, Slade felt, have really graced the popular Gilbert and Sullivan operetta, so far as looks were concerned. She was not very large. Her bright head came hardly to his shoulder. Her hair was a smoldering flame haloing a small, oval-shaped face with high cheek bones that gave her astonishingly large eyes an illusory upward slant at the corners that was almost Mongolian. They were green as emeralds, very alert eyes with a hint of hardness in their clear depths that Slade thought was at variance with the

9

softly curved, vividly red mouth below the little straight nose.

The face was arresting, but it was her costume that occasioned the Ranger's remark to himself. She wore small half-boots of softly tanned leather and tightly fitting black pantaloons that came barely halfway between hip and thigh. Her black silk shirt, mannish in cut, was open at the throat. Around her left shoulder was looped a heavy leather whip, the lash of which was a good ten feet in length—a regular mule skinner's whip. The black handle rested in the soft "V" between the proud upthrust of her beautifully rounded breasts.

"Reckon I could," Slade answered her question; he was getting the drift of things. Evidently his range tramp appearance was even more convincing than he thought.

"You can get all you want to eat here," the girl said. Slade held back a smile.

"Ma'am, I'm not in the habit of accepting handouts from ladies," he replied.

"I'm not offering you charity," the girl snapped at him. "This place needs cleaning up. There's a broom, and a bucket and a mop in the kitchen. I just whipped the swamper out of here for getting drunk on the job. Get to work and you can have all you want to eat, and a few dollars besides. I've a notion you can use both. Incidentally, I'm not a lady. I'm Francia, and I own this place. Most people consider I'm a hellcat and—other things. Perhaps I'm both, but don't make the mistake of jumping to conclusions too fast; it isn't healthy. Well, what do you say?"

Slade's mind had been working swiftly as she spoke. The offer did not lack attractions. It would give him the needed excuse for sticking around the section. Might even be better than a chore of riding, which he had planned to tie on to. His movements would be less restricted, and he would be much less apt to attract attention—nobody ever paid any attention to a swamper pushing a mop. In addition, it might provide opportunity to glean valuable information. If Captain Jim knew what he was talking about, and he usually did, Slade knew he had no light chore ahead of him, but one fraught with difficulty and danger that might even tax the powers of El Halcón, Captain Jim's Lieutenant and ace-man.

"Okay," he replied to Francia, "I'll take the chore, for a while."

"Oh, I don't expect you to stay long," the girl answered. "You won't be happy without a horse between your legs, whether you're working or not. Sit down at that vacant table over there and I'll have the cook send you in a good meal. You'll work better after you've lined your belly."

Slade hung his battered hat on a peg and sat down at the table. His gaze fixed on Francia, and he humorously half wondered if he was still out on the desert, and plagued by a tantalizing mirage.

But the meal a waiter brought him a little later was real enough, and a darned good one, and there was plenty of it. He ate it all and felt much better despite the fatigue that was approaching the verge of exhaustion. He rolled a cigarette with his left hand and smoked thoughtfully, his eyes following Francia as she moved about, lithe and graceful as a panther.

His eyes were slightly puzzled as he watched her. She just didn't seem to make sense, seemed utterly out of place.

A girl running a cowtown saloon! And such a girl. Were she an Amazonic old heifer like Big-nose Kate, Razor-back Molly, or Wingless Angel Sue, who had been known to take on such a chore, it would be understandable. But a fresh-faced little beauty with a figure that left nothing to be desired. How, he wondered, did she keep order when the usual hell busted loose. He was soon to learn.

Francia was coming in his direction. He stood up and, to his surprise, weaved a little on his feet, a fluttery mist forming before his eyes; he was a devil of a sight tireder than he had thought. However, his eyes cleared before she reached him, and he grew firm on his feet.

Nevertheless, she gave him a searching glance and the emerald eyes were speculative. She seemed to hesitate.

"Guess I'm all set to go to work, Ma'am," he told her.

Francia still seemed to hesitate. Slade glanced at her expectantly.

"All right," she said, and led the way to the kitchen, the seductive sway of her hips causing him to forget some of his weariness.

In the kitchen she gestured to a peg beside the stove. "Take your guns off and hang them there," she said. "They don't go well with a bucket and a mop."

It was Slade's turn to hesitate. Asking El Halcón to go without his guns was tantamount to asking him to go without

11

his pants. However, he capitulated in deference to the role
he had decided to assume. Swampers didn't usually pack
Colt Forty-fives when working.

"Start with the kitchen and the lunch counter," Francia
said, "and try to keep out of the customers' way."

Slade cleaned up the kitchen. He did the chore as he did
everything he set his hand to—well. The old cook nodded
approvingly.

"First time this place has looked decent in a week," he
said. "That tramp Francia ran out last night was a born work
dodger." Slade nodded, refilled his bucket and tackled the
lunch counter. He glanced about and spotted Francia nearby
at the edge of the dance floor. Something was apparently
out of order there. A big cowhand, more than half drunk, was
pawing one of the dance-floor girls, obnoxiously. Francia
reached out and jerked his hand away.

"Stop it!" she ordered. "Behave yourself like a gentleman,
or get out."

The puncher turned, his eyes glowing. "Okay, baby, you
got her beat anyhow," he said, and reached for Francia. She
glided back lithely a few steps, her fingers on the handle of
the whip.

"Keep away," she warned.

The puncher lunged for her. Slade took a half step in his
direction.

But Francia didn't need him. The long lash spun from her
shoulder and hissed through the air. It circled the cowboy's
waist with a sharp crack, cutting through his shirt like a
knife. It came away stained red.

The man gave a scream of pain and reached for his gun.
Slade tensed for the leap that would be as the forward bound
of a mountain lion, and just as lethal.

But Francia still didn't need him or anybody else. The lash
whizzed out and coiled around the puncher's wrist like a con-
stricting snake, spinning the gun from his hand; blood spurted.
Francia jerked with all the strength of her lithe young body.
With another howl the man crashed to the floor on his face.
And Francia went to work on him with the whip.

Slade's flesh crawled a little as the lash hissed and sang.
Francia's red lips were slightly parted, showing the gleam
of white little teeth. The green eyes were hard and she wielded
the whip in an impersonal way, like to an automaton respond-

12

ing to perfectly meshed gears. But Slade sensed that she didn't particularly enjoy the performance and, quite likely was the only person in the room who felt so. She ruled by terror, as it were. Let such a situation get out of hand and she was through. Doubtless the dealers and waiters would come to her aid were it really necessary, but then her prestige would be gone and she would constantly be in for real trouble. But why, he wondered, did she wear that bizarre costume that was in itself provocative of trouble.

A half dozen licks and the fellow was howling for mercy. Francia drew back. Two impassive dealers politely escorted the groaning, cursing puncher to the door. Francia turned, and came face to face with Slade.

"See how I handle things?" she said. "Be wise and keep it in mind."

"Yes?" Just a monosyllable, but its effect on the red-haired girl was remarkable. For an instant she faced him, defiantly, but something in the cold, pale eyes boring into hers caused her to abruptly turn away. She headed for the kitchen, and her shoulders shook a little, almost as if she were shivering. Slade went back to work.

In the kitchen, Francia held converse with old Stiffy, the cook.

"Stiffy," she said, "were you ever scared?"

"Oh, I suppose so, but I never seemed to find it out," Stiffy returned cheerfully. "Why?"

"Because," Francia said slowly, "a minute ago I was."

"Of that horned toad you whipped?"

Francia shook her bright head. "No," she said slowly, "of that tall swamper I just hired. It was his eyes. I never saw such eyes. They seemed to look right through me, and right inside. I'm not wearing many clothes, but they stripped me naked. Naked to my bones, and—and my soul. I—I wonder if they found anything of which they didn't approve?"

"That's a question for you to answer, and I've a notion *they've* got the answer already," said Stiffy. "Yep, I noticed 'em, too. When he came into the kitchen they looked me up and down and I got the same feeling that they were looking right inside of me, and if there were any dark places I'd rather cover up, they'd search 'em out. I've got some dark places, all right, but they were paid up long ago, so I don't worry too much. Then all of a sudden he smiled and the

13

look in the eyes changed. Was just like the sun looking down at me from a blue sky and made me feel all warm and cozy inside. Yes, he's a strange feller."

"He didn't smile at me," Francia murmured. "Chuck-line rider, isn't he?"

Stiffy shook his wise old head. "Nope, he ain't and never has been. He's done cow chambermaiding in his time but not much for quite a while. Marks of rope and branding iron are mighty faint. But I noticed something else."

"What?" Francia asked.

"Calluses."

"Calluses?"

"Yep, on his thumbs and first fingers. The kind of calluses the hammers and triggers of guns make when they're drawn time after time, week after week, and month after month. You've got a quick-draw two-gun man working for you, Francia."

"I wonder what he's here for?" Francia remarked.

"Hard to tell," Stiffy replied. "His sort is kinda unpredictable. Could be just passin' through, but somehow I got a notion he isn't."

Francia gazed across the room, apparently at nothing. "Stiffy," she said, "I have the strangest feeling that before he leaves here my brother will sleep better."

"Could be," Stiffy conceded, soberly. "Think it would be a good notion to tell him the story?"

"I don't see how it could do any harm, and it might do some good," Francia said slowly. The green eyes looked contemplative.

"I've got a notion he'd be really good looking with a shave," she remarked inconsequentially. "He's not bad even with that stubble on his face."

Stiffy's blue and very keen eyes shot her an amused glance.

"You can't tame that sort with a whip," he said with apparent irrelevance. "You'd likely end up getting a taste of it yourself."

The contemplative look intensified. "I wonder how it would be, used by the right man?"

Stiffy shook with silent laughter. "Judging from the way that gent squalled tonight, not so good," he answered.

"He wasn't a girl."

14

"So I figure," Stiffy agreed.

A waiter hurrying in with an order ended a conversation that had continued long enough.

THREE

ACCUSTOMED AS HE WAS to watching doors, no matter how hectic the moment, Slade saw the two men enter as Francia went to work on the cowboy. They paused inside the door and appeared to enjoy the performance. One was tall, broad-shouldered, finely set up. He had tawny hair, clear blue eyes and a lean, deeply bronzed face. His mouth, above a square chin, was well shaped; the lips a trifle too full, a trifle too red, perhaps. When they drew back in a grin of enjoyment as he watched the whipping, they were a thin line against white teeth.

His companion was small and dark. His glittering black eyes, set deep in almost cavernous sockets, seemed to look every way at once. His mouth was hard and slightly pulled down at the corners.

Both men wore rangeland garb and packed guns. After the beaten cowboy was ushered out, they sauntered to a table and sat down. The big man beckoned a waiter. Slade had a notion he was a ranch owner, the other his range boss. Later he was to learn that his surmise was correct.

The babble of talk that had hushed during the episode resumed. The orchestra struck up a sprightly tune. Boots thumped and French heels clicked on the dance floor. What had happened was apparently forgotten. Slade kept on working.

The aftermath of the excitement had set in and his weariness had redoubled; his movements were a bit uncertain. He finished with the lunch counter and worked out into the room toward the table where the big, tawny-haired man sat talking to his black-eyed companion. Just as he reached it he made an awkward stab at the bucket with the mop. The bucket overturned and dirty water sloshed over the big man's boots. Trying to retrieve it, Slade floundered off balance. The big man leaped to his feet with an oath and smashed Slade on the side of the jaw. Slade went down.

A close observer well versed in such matters would have noted that Slade was riding with the punch and that he fell light, taking his weight on the palms of his hands. He got up, rather slowly. The other stood waiting, fists clenched, a sneer twisting his lips.

For an instant El Halcón was tempted to give the gentleman the larrupin' he had coming, but that would have been out of character with the role he had chosen to assume. And anyhow, Francia was instantly in front of him.

"That will be all, Sid," she told the big man. "I won't have you slapping my help around. That will be all, I said." Her fingers toyed with the handle of the whip as she spoke. Across the room, the lookout got down from his high stool and strolled toward the table, the twin muzzles of his cocked, sawed-off shotgun looking hungry.

The big man shrugged and sat down. "Okay, Francia," he said, "but keep that awkward range tramp out of my way."

Francia turned to Slade. "Be more careful hereafter," she admonished. "Take your bucket to the kitchen and sit down. You've done enough for one night. I'll see you in a little while."

Slade did as she said. At the kitchen door he found old Stiffy, the cook, standing outside. Stiffy grinned, and winked at him.

In the kitchen Slade sat down and rolled a cigarette, his fingers trembling a little from weariness. He was not in the best of tempers and he would not forget the man who hit him without real cause. Then his sense of humor came to his rescue and he grinned, a trifle wryly.

"Control yourself even in the moment of provocation when it is expedient to do so," says the "Book" of the Rangers. He felt that he had obeyed the very sensible admonition.

Francia had paused at the kitchen door beside Stiffy. "I wonder," she said slowly, "why didn't he fight back?"

"Ma'am," Stiffy replied dryly, "You just saw a plumb fine example of self control. If he'd chose to do so, he'd have taken Sid Gholen apart quicker than I can slice a ham. For some reason he didn't want to. Why? I ain't got the least notion."

16

Meanwhile, Slade was the subject of conversation in another part of the room.

"Gholen, that was wrong," the little black-eyed man said to his companion. "Why do you always have to fly off the handle for no good reason? You're smart and you're educated and you know how to do things most people don't, and you figure things out fine as frog hair, but you're too blasted good at getting your bristles up like you did this evening. Funny thing how a feller who can handle men like you do can't handle himself. You made a bad enemy tonight for no good reason."

"That yellow range tramp!" Gholen scoffed. "You didn't see him fight back, did you, Crane?"

"No," Crane admitted, "but if you'd used your eyes and head, you might have seen why. The man is sick or something. I watched him cross the room. He was stumbling and barely able to stay on his feet."

"Drunk, more likely," Gholen said.

"I don't think he was drunk," Crane replied. "And he's got bad eyes."

Gholen grunted, and changed the subject.

Slade had just finished his cigarette when Francia entered the kitchen.

"I'm sorry for what happened," she said. "Sid Gholen has a nasty temper, but he owns one of the best spreads in the section and he's a good customer."

Slade merely nodded. Francia speculated him a moment. "I had a good idea when I told you to leave your guns in here," she said. "I'm glad you didn't have them when Gholen hit you."

Slade's eyes crinkled a little at the corners. "Who said I'd have gone for my guns?" he asked mildly.

"Nobody," Francia replied, "but I've a feeling you would have. And you'd doubtless have gotten yourself killed. Plenty of folks will tell you Sid Gholen has the fastest gunhand in Texas."

Slade's lips quirked a little, but he refrained from comment. Old Stiffy grinned.

Francia glanced around the spotless kitchen approvingly. "You'll do," she said. "By the way, what's your name?"

"Most everybody calls me Walt," Slade replied.

"Okay, Walt," she nodded. The green eyes looked him up and down. "Where are you going to sleep?" she asked.

"Been sleeping under the stars quite a bit of late," Slade replied evasively in the interest of his deception.

"So I gathered," she said dryly. "There's a bed in the back room over behind the end of the bar. The other swamper slept there. I'll change the sheets and blankets."

She left the kitchen. "Go to the bar and have a drink on the house," she said over her shoulder.

Slade had the drink. He felt that he needed it. As he sipped the glass he studied the room, noting that Sid Gholen and his companion were nowhere in sight. Before he had emptied his glass, Francia reappeared.

"I'm going upstairs to change," she said. "Have another drink if you want it."

Slade didn't particularly want the second drink, but he ordered his glass refilled. It would give him further opportunity to estimate the crowd until she returned.

So far as he could see, it was a rather typical cowtown bunch, nothing particularly outstanding about any of them, although he quickly concluded that quite a few of those present, while they quite probably had once been cowhands, had not worked at it for some time. Not remarkable, though; Olton was in the nature of a crossroads and the recipient of all sorts. Which was of interest to the Ranger.

Francia came down shortly. Now faded "Levi's" had replaced the short pantaloons. They set off the alluring curves of her slender form almost as well as did her former costume, Slade thought approvingly. He noted that a cartridge belt encircled her astonishingly small waist. From the belt hung a business-like looking gun. The ever-present whip was around her shoulder.

"Want your pay tonight, or do you figure to stay on a while?" she asked.

"Reckon I'll stay on a while," Slade replied laconically.

"Okay," Francia said. "See you tomorrow afternoon. Stiffy will tell you what to do till I get here."

"Going for a ride," Slade asked curiously.

"Yes, out to my ranchhouse. I own a spread twelve miles up the valley."

"And you're taking a twelve-mile ride at this time of night, alone?"

"I can take care of myself," Francia replied, a bit defiantly, he thought.

"Possibly," he conceded, but his voice did not carry conviction.

Francia looked at him, but once again it was her gaze that shifted first. She turned on her heel. "Good night," she said, over her shoulder. "You'd better go to bed. You look all in."

She walked lithely from the saloon, looking neither to right nor left. Slade placed his half emptied glass on the bar and headed for the back room. Francia had the right of it; he was darn close to being all in. He paused at the kitchen to retrieve his guns. Reaching the room, he closed the door and glanced about.

The room was small but spotlessly clean, and showed signs of having been mopped and dusted in the past hour. The soft glow of a bracket light revealed the neatly turned back sheets and the pillow of the narrow bed to be snowy white.

"The first thing that really looks like a bed for nearly a week," he told the big sixes, as he examined them carefully to make sure they had suffered no harm during the trip across the desert through the storm. "And she made it herself! The idea of that hellcat making a bed."

Just before he dropped into dreamless sleep, he chuckled aloud, "Oh, she's a hellcat, all right, or pretends to be. But blazes! what a shape she's got!"

FOUR

WHEN HE AWAKENED the following mid morning, Slade did not immediately get up. He was his normal self again and his mind was clear, so he proceeded to do a little serious thinking. He recalled his interview with Captain Jim McNelty, the famous Commander of the Border Battalion of the Texas Rangers. Captain Jim had been in a very bad temper.

"It's a roving bunch of the worst sort," he rumbled. "Well

led, well organized, intelligent and deadly. They've robbed three banks, wrecked and robbed a train, held up three stage coaches, killed three or four people. All in widely separated sections. Complaints have been pouring in and the governor wants to know why the Rangers don't do something about it. Local authorities appear to be helpless. The hellions hit and run and are across county lines before the blasted sheriffs can get off their rumps and after them. Yes, a roving bunch —they've been swallerforking over seventeen counties, more or less. But in my opinion they have a headquarters somewhere, a hole-up where they can lie low for a time before staging another raid. Might be hiding behind a quite respectable front somewhere. And I'd say it's somewhere in the Trans-Pecos, a bit north of the Big Bend country—they've been steadily heading in that direction."

"Sounds logical," Slade admitted.

"Okay," said Captain Jim. "Get going and see what you can do. If you get scared, let me know and I'll amble over to lend a hand."

"I'll do that, sir," Slade promised. They chuckled together, mutually appreciating the joke.

"Be careful of yourself, Walt," was Captain Jim's final admonishment. Don't take unnecessary chances, and for Pete's sake try not to pose as El Halcón if you can keep from it. That fool business gives me the creeps when I think of it. Someday it'll cause you to get your comeuppance from some trigger-happy deputy or marshal, or some gun-slinging hellion out to acquire a reputation and not beyond shooting in the back to get it."

"Really, sir, I think your fears are exaggerated," Slade protested. "It's not so bad as all that, and being looked upon as only El Halcón, one of their own sort, sometimes causes owlhoots to get careless. Which wouldn't be the case if they knew me to be a Ranger. And it opens up avenues of information that would otherwise be closed."

Captain Jim didn't look convinced, but he said no more at the moment, except, "Well, good hunting!"

Due to his habit of working under cover as much as possible and often not revealing his Ranger connections, Walt Slade had built up an unusual dual reputation. Those who knew he was a Ranger were wont to declare that he was

20

the ablest as well as the most fearless of the illustrious body of law enforcement officers. Others, who knew him only as El Halcón, insisted he was a blasted owlhoot too smart to get caught, so far, but who'd end up dancing on nothing at the end of a rope, sooner or later.

All of which provided Slade with a certain amount of amusement. So he went his carefree way as El Halcón, his dark eyes looking out on the world with cheerful anticipation, and finding it good.

"I think I'll take a train to Van Horn and then ride west by north into the Trans-Pecos region," he observed meditatively.

"A good notion," agreed Captain Jim. "So far as I've been able to learn, the hellions came from there and, as I said, appear to be headed back in that direction, raising the devil as they go. I'll have a stall car hooked onto the morning local for your horse. So get going, and take care of yourself."

Slade enjoyed a rather long but comfortable train ride. As he gazed out the window at the varied scenery flitting past, he conned over what Captain Jim had told him. Such raids as the aforementioned were not uncommon, but this one, which had set a good portion of south Texas in an uproar, was about the most ambitious he could recall. Somebody with brains, audacity and imagination was engineering it.

Well, he'd gone up against such outfits before. So he continued to enjoy the scenery with a peaceful mind.

From time to time he dozed, rousing up when the train paused at various stations like Sanderson, set in a deep canyon, one wall of which rose over the main street. It had been a wild frontier town and was still far from tame. Outlaws roamed the mountains and canyons of the Big Bend country to the southwest, and trafficked in "wet" herds stolen in Mexico and driven across the Rio Grande, and found diversion in Sanderson. The famous Judge Roy Bean had a saloon there, from which he dispensed justice in a most unorthodox manner, a law book in one hand, a sixgun in the other.

More wayside stops, mountains looming closer. To the southwest the far-flung ramparts of the Big Bend wilderness, directly ahead the first of the ranges that formed the mountain barrier of the Trans-Pecos area.

Then Marathon, the gateway to the Big Bend, treeless, arid, mountain-bound. A town of unpainted adobe houses,

21

the main supply center for the vast ranching country extending almost across the six thousand square miles of Brewster County, larger than some eastern states.

Alpine, cradled in a valley between towering mountains, a desert beginning at the end of its streets. Marfa, treeless, jacal-fringed. More rumbling and snorting and jangling of couplers. Then Van Horn.

At Van Horn, Slade released Shadow from his cramped quarters, saddled up and rode west, following a faint trail that paralleled the railroad and at no great distance from the right-of-way. And rode into trouble.

Directly ahead was a broad arid valley lying between the frowning ramparts of the Sierra Diablo on the west and the Deleware Mountains on the east, traversing one of the most desolate but weirdly beautiful stretches of country to be found in Texas. The vegetation was sage, greasewood, prickly pear, yucca and Octillo. The salt encrusted shore lines of salt lakes gleamed like hazy silver ribbons. In the mountains was a tangle of ridges and deep narrow canyons, where there were mines—lost and active. The mountains loomed stark against the deep blue of the sky, their crests glowing in the sunlight. A wild and austere land.

But farther to the north, Slade knew, were narrow valleys luxuriantly grassed where cows became fat and frisky in no time.

Mile after mile he rode, hoping to glean from some scattered settlement, lone ranch or mining activity, information relative to the outlaw bunch he sought.

Distant in the west sounded the whistle of an eastbound passenger train. The trail climbed a slope that almost overhung the right-of-way. The railroad, however, was hidden by a straggle of growth.

The whistle sounded again, much nearer. Shadow, ambling along sedately, was not far from the crest of the rise. The rumble of the approaching train could now be heard. It grew louder and louder, the exhaust pounding, the side rods clanking.

Abruptly the whistle shrieked again. The boom of the exhaust shut off. There was a clang-jangle of brake rigging, the screech of the shoes against the wheels. Then a terrific crash, a bellow of escaping steam, followed almost immediately by a crackle of shots that continued like an explod-

22

ing pack of fire crackers. Slade's voice rang out, "Trail Shadow, trail!"

Instantly the great black lunged forward, spurning the surface of the trail with flying hoofs. He foamed to the crest of the rise. Slade pulled him to a halt and sat staring.

Directly below and some three hundred yards distant was a scene of destruction, violence and wild excitement. The locomotive lay on its side at the bottom of the embankment, steam pouring from broken pipes. Scattered around were crossties, and boulders that had been heaped on the track at the apex of the curve. The express car, its front wheels off the iron, teetered on the embankment edge.

And crouched behind some low bushes a dozen men blazed away at the express car and the coach windows. The boom of the shots, the rumble of the escaping steam and the frightened cries of passengers rose in a thin jumble of sound to where the Ranger sat his horse.

Something sailed from behind one of the bushes, trailing smoke and sparks. The dynamite exploded against the express-car door, shattering it. The wreckers whooped with delight and redoubled their fire.

Slade slid his heavy Winchester from the saddle boot, clamped the butt to his shoulder. His eyes glanced along the sights and he squeezed the trigger.

The rifle wisped smoke. One of the wreckers leaped into the air and pitched forward on his face. Slade shifted the muzzle a trifle and fired again. A second outlaw fell sideways to lie motionless. Slade let out a series of yells and emptied the magazine as fast as he could pull trigger—the ejection lever a flashing blur—to simulate several long guns going off at once. He shoved fresh cartridges into the magazine with frantic speed. The wreckers fired in return, but they were using sixguns and the distance was great; save one that ripped through his hatbrim, no slugs came close.

A man ran toward one of the horses, doubtless to procure a rifle. The Winchester muzzle followed him, spurted smoke. His right arm flashed wildly and Slade could almost hear his yelp of pain.

That was enough for the wreckers. They made a concerted rush for their horses, swung into the saddles and sped west at a gallop. All save two who lay without sound or movement.

Slade speeded them on their way with bullets. He watched

intently to see if they would turn and ride up the trail. However, they did not. They swerved across it some distance beyond the bottom of the slope and continued north, quickly vanishing among the trees and thickets. Slade watched for a moment to make sure they had no intention of returning. He made no attempt to follow them. Did they realize that they had but one man to deal with, they would turn on him, and odds of ten to one were a bit lopsided.

Below, people were pouring from the coaches, shouting and waving their hands. Slade waved back and sent Shadow down the slope. At the bottom of the sag he turned onto the right-of-way.

A blue-clad trainman came running to meet him. "Blazes! cowboy, you showed up at a good time," he called. Slade nodded and glanced toward the overturned locomotive.

"How about the engineer and fireman?" he asked. "Are they badly hurt?"

"Just banged up a bit, nothing serious," the conductor replied. "The express messenger was stunned by the dynamite, but he's coming out of it. Which he wouldn't be doing right now if it wasn't for you. The blankety-blanks would have shot him, sure as blazes."

"Probably," Slade conceded. "Everybody else okay?"

"Guess so, except for some cuts and bruises," the conductor replied.

"Money in the express car?" Slade asked.

"Guess so, a bank shipment," added the trainman. "Messenger was trying to fight 'em off, but he wouldn't have had any luck. Some fellers with you up there? Sounded like it." Slade shook his head.

The conductor whistled. "Feller, you're good!" he exclaimed. Slade changed the subject.

"Have you a portable telegraph instrument on your train?" he asked. "If so, we'll hook it up and notify Van Horn so they can have a wreck train sent to take care of things. Can you send? If you can't, I can."

"Reckon I can tap out enough to get by," the conductor replied. "Only I don't know how we'll hook it up." He glanced dubiously at the row of telegraph poles marching along parallel to the tracks. "Them poles are mighty tall."

"Get the instrument and wire, I'll take care of the pole," Slade told him, swinging down from the saddle.

A few minutes later the conductor and others shook their heads in admiration.

"Going up it like a squirrel," chuckled the conductor. "Say, he's some feller!"

"You can say that double," declared the grizzled engineer, rubbing a bruised head. "And such shooting! Never saw anything like it. Wonder who the devil is he?"

"Doesn't matter," said the conductor. "He's the bully boy with a glass eye for my money."

Slade hooked up the instrument and descended. Soon a message to Van Horn was clicking over the wires.

"Tell them to notify the sheriff and have him come out here," Slade directed. "I want him to look over those two bodies and dispose of them."

The conductor nodded and worked the key.

Slade himself looked over the two bodies, the conductor beside him, and found nothing of interest save considerable money, which he replaced. They were ordinary-appearing individuals with nothing to distinguish them. Their clothes and their guns were regulation rangeland.

"Recognize either of them?" he asked the conductor. The trainman shook his head.

"Never saw either of the skunks," he replied.

Quizzing the passengers who crowded around also produced negative results. Which was what Slade expected.

The dead wreckers' horses were good-looking animals, their rigs commonplace. Slade thought that the brand of one was an East Texas burn, but he wasn't sure. Meant nothing. Horses can be bought, traded or stolen. And owlhoots often slick-ironed unregistered brands that could not be traced; the sheriff could take charge of them, too.

"Well, reckon I'll be riding," he told the conductor. "Nothing more I can do here."

"But aren't you going to wait for the sheriff?" protested the railroader. "And I've a notion the express people will want to hand you a little appreciation for what you saved them. Messenger tells me there's better'n thirty thousand dollars in the safe."

"You fellows take it and have a bust," Slade smiled. "No, I can't wait. I have a chore to attend to. Be seeing you."

"Golly, but he's a tall feller," the conductor remarked as they watched him ride west. "Shoulders and a chest to go

25

with his height. And his eyes! I never saw such eyes. Go through you like a greased knife. Well, whoever he is, he's okay. They don't come any better."

There were emphatic nods of agreement from all present.

When Slade reached the point where the outlaws had crossed the trail, he turned north in their wake.

"Looks like maybe we made a mite of a start," he remarked to Shadow. "Oh, it's the bunch we're after, no doubt in my mind as to that. And they're headed north by west, just as I expected. Yes, their headquarters is up there somewhere in the Trans-Pecos region. Well, maybe we can get a line on where they went."

He didn't. Soon the trail led to a range of low hills that were criss-crossed with trails, old and new, any of which the outlaws could have followed. Finally he gave up in disgust and rode on north by west through the dying light.

The next two days were barren of results. Nobody could give him any information concerning the bunch, nor had any depredations been committed in the section, so far as he could learn.

Then the ill-advised attempt to take a short-cut across the Tinaja Desert without making due allowance for the weather vagaries of that unpredictable terrain, and his subsequent arrival at Olton in sorry case, followed.

FIVE

AND AS HE RELAXED comfortably in the bed Francia had made, he wondered if his hunch was a straight one, and that if here in this turbulent cow-country section the outlaw bunch he was trailing had their headquarters.

He was impressed by the fact that although he had circled about a lot and covered a great deal of territory since losing the trail many miles east and south of the desert, nobody he contacted could recall seeing such a bunch; and he heard of no depredations being committed since the abortive attempt to rob the express car.

It was this last that inclined Slade to believe that their hide-out was indeed somewhere in the section, for it was logical to think that they would hardly pull something spectacular when approaching their home grounds. Once they got settled and felt secure from pursuit, they would no doubt cut loose again. So, as usual, his hunch, so called, was based on sound reasoning.

He chuckled as his thoughts turned to Francia. Undoubtedly her place was a gathering point. If nothing else, the bizarre costume she wore, added to her personal appearance, would attract the curious. So his position, unusual for El Halcón, as a swamper in a saloon, might pay off handsomely in the end. There was a good chance that he might catch an incautious word, or two, dropped in his presence. Nobody gave a swamper much thought, especially one well versed in being unobtrusive. He yawned, stretched and leaped out of bed.

"Got your breakfast all ready and waiting for you," said old Stiffy, when he appeared in the kitchen. "Francia said you are not to go to work until evening, when she shows up. Not much business in the daytime and we got a day swamper who is all right, an old Mexican who, like myself, was here when her brother ran the diggin'."

"Her brother?" Slade prompted, as Stiffy poured him a cup of coffee.

"Yep, that's right," nodded Stiffy. "Her brother Tom Renshaw, a nice jigger, opened this place and made a go of it. About six months back he got himself killed by three hellions who held up the place. He also owned the Rocking T spread, to the north of here, and that day he'd sold a herd. Had the money right here in the safe. Him and Sid Gholen had run their herds together and the money Sid got for his cows was here, too. Well, just at closing time, when there was nobody here but Tom and me, those three devils, two big ones and a little one with handkerchiefs tied over their faces bulged in. Two of them had their guns out and ready for business. Tom made the mistake of reaching under the bar. The big one who didn't have his gun out pulled and shot him between the eyes. The other big one let me have it and

27

creased me. When I came to, Tom was dead and the money was gone, and so were the three killers."

"Wasn't the safe locked?" Slade asked.

"Uh-huh, it was when they came in," Stiffy replied. "But when I got my senses back it was standing wide open and empty as a cowhand's pocket the day after payday."

"Did they blow it?" The old cook shook his head.

"Nope. Didn't blow it, didn't jimmy it. Worked the combination slick as a whistle."

"Unusual for this part of the country," Slade commented.

"Uh-huh," Stiffy agreed, "but all sorts have been sliding through here since the railroad came along, a few years back."

Slade nodded and looked expectant. Stiffy went on with his story.

"Judge Arbuckle, who handled Tom's legal business, had his sister's address. He wrote her, informing her of Tom's death and asking what he should do about the property, seeing as she was Tom Renshaw's only known kin. She wrote back that she was coming over here from Arizona to look after it. Ten days later she rode in, dressed like she was when she left last night. We all figured she'd sell out, and Sid Gholen was all set to buy. Reckon he wasn't much interested in the saloon, but the spread joins with his land and would round out his holding. But she 'lowed to run the place. Everybody thought it was a prime joke, a pretty young girl running a salty cowtown saloon; but mighty soon they stopped laughing. First day she took charge, one of the dealers tried to get fresh with her. Well, she drilled a bullet through that gent's arm with that gun she packs and did it pronto. He's the feller who handles the big poker game in the corner, and I reckon right now he'd kill anybody who really did anything to her. That was the starter."

"Something of a starter, I'd say," Slade chuckled.

"Uh-huh," Stiffy agreed, "but that wasn't nothing. Two days later she showed up in those short pants and with that mule skinner's whip over her shoulder. She used the whip on a couple of the gents, and used it proper. Hasn't had to use it for a long time until last night. She hit the swamper a couple of light licks when she run him out, but that drunk last night, a stranger to the place, was the first she's really worked over for quite a spell. Oh, she's considerable of a gal. She's known all over the section now and this place

28

does twice the business of any other in town. She runs an absolutely square place and she's swell to the help. There isn't a jigger working here who wouldn't fight for her at the drop of a hat. Not that she's liable to need anybody to do her fighting for her. She can take care of herself."

Slade was inclined to agree, with reservations.

"She's a mighty good-looking girl, though, don't you think?" Stiffy asked, his gaze fixed on a shining copper pot that hung behind the big range.

"She is," Slade said, and meant it.

"Figure you'll stick around for a spell?"

"Possibly."

"I've a notion Francia would like for you to," Stiffy said, still intent on the pot.

"Well," Slade smiled, "although perhaps I shouldn't say it, I believe I did a better chore of cleaning up than did my predecessor."

Stiffy regarded the pot severely, and indulged in a cryptic remark. "I'd say you did a better chore here than any man who's stepped in here since she took over," he said.

The little devils of laughter that always seemed to lurk in the back of Slade's eyes suddenly leaped to the front. He knew that while he discoursed in an offhand manner, the old man was studying him, and doing a bit of probing. Slade also had noted a few things of interest. Every now and then, in an absentminded fashion, Stiffy's hand would rise to caress the left lapel of the loose white linen coat he wore. Also, his eyes, set deep in a network of wrinkles, were very light blue in color, with a quick glitter in their depths. The kind of eyes accredited to Billy the Kid, Doc Holliday, Buckskin Frank Leslie and other famous gunfighters of the Old West. Slade decided to do a little probing on his own account.

"Where'd you learn to cook?" he asked abruptly.

Stiffy abandoned the pot, glanced at Slade and grinned slightly.

"In a nice big kitchen about the size of this whole joint," he replied. "Wore my hair short in those days, and didn't go out at night."

Slade nodded his understanding. "I haven't learned there —yet," he remarked.

"Try not to," said Stiffy. "You wouldn't enjoy it."

29

"I'll try not to," Slade promised. Stiffy nodded, then shot out an unexpected and apparently irrelevant remark.

"Don't underestimate Sid Gholen. He ain't got no feeling in his trigger finger, and that range boss of his, Alf Crane, is just as bad and, I sometimes think, smarter."

"Thanks for the good advice," Slade answered. "I won't forget it. This place makes out pretty well, doesn't it?"

"Sure does," Stiffy agreed. "Francia would be settin' pretty if it wasn't for that blasted spread."

"What's wrong with the spread?"

"Nothing," Stiffy replied. "It's a darn good holding, but there's a mortgage, and she's been losing cows ever since she took over. And just a month back her range boss, old Preston Bates, who was with Tom before her, got himself shot."

"Who shot him?"

"That's what the sheriff and some other folks would like to know. He was found over close to where a trail runs under some cliffs to the west, on Sid Gholen's Swinging J land."

"Looks like he might have stumbled onto something off-color," Slade commented.

"Could be," the cook conceded. "There were hoof marks around, quite a few of 'em, as if a bunch of cows had passed that way."

Slade nodded. "The Rocking T and the Swinging J join, you say?"

"Uh-huh. The Swinging J is west of the Rocking T. It's a good holding. To the east is old Jackson Haynes's J Bar H, the biggest holding in the section. Several more spreads to the north and east. It's a good cow country. Good for rustlers, too. Everybody's been losing cows during the past six months. That is, until about a month ago. Then the wide-looping all of a sudden stopped. Expect the hellions will cut loose again before long, though."

With which Slade was in agreement.

"Where do you figure the cows go?" he asked.

"West, and then north to New Mexico, I reckon," Stiffy replied. "Rough country over there."

"Not southwest to the Rio Grande and Mexico—that's the better market for stolen beef?"

"Across near fifty miles of desert without water? Cows couldn't do it."

Slade nodded again, but did not comment. He pushed back his empty plate, got up and sauntered across the kitchen to gaze out the window. Abruptly he turned to face Stiffy, who had also gotten up and was pottering about the stove.

"Stiffy, did you get a look at the men who robbed the place and killed Tom Renshaw?" he asked. Stiffy shook his head.

"As I told you, they had handkerchiefs tied over their faces; but I noticed something about the one who shot Tom that I'll never forget. The way he pulled his gun was sorta funny. He was fast, mighty fast, but he tipped the muzzle of the gun up as it cleared the leather instead of jutting it straight forward as most everybody does. Looks like he shoots for the head. As I said, Preston Bates, the range boss, was shot between the eyes just like Tom was. I feel pretty sure the feller who killed Bates was the feller who killed Tom."

"Not much to go on, but something," Slade admitted.

"So I'm waiting for a feller who tips his gun muzzle up instead of shoving it forward," Stiffy said, the glitter in his eyes intensified.

"And if you meet him?" Slade asked curiously.

Stiffy's hands moved, the left gripping the lapel of his white coat, the right blurring across his chest. At the same instant he spun around sideways on his heel. A short-barreled Smith & Weston menaced Slade. He was fast, blinding fast. Slade's eyes grew reflective as the Smith slid back into its sheath.

"Never saw a draw just like that before," he remarked. "Never heard of one like it but once. Some oldtimers were talking about famous gun slingers like John Ringo, Curly Bill Brocius, Doc Holliday and—Buckskin Frank Leslie. One described how Leslie used a cross-pull and spun around sideways at the same time so as to present a smaller target. He said he never saw a similar draw and never heard of anybody else using it. Seems it was Leslie's private invention."

"That so?" Stiffy replied cheerfully. "Lots of folks will tell you that Buckskin Frank died quite a while back, after he got out of the penitentiary."

"So I've heard," Slade admitted. "At least he sure dropped plumb out of sight. Let's see, Buckskin Frank would be about sixty now, if he was alive."

"Uh-huh, guess he would," Stiffy agreed. "If he was alive."

31

Slade had instinctively buckled on his guns before he left the back room. Now he stepped back a pace.

"Suppose you try it again," he suggested.

Stiffy tried. But before his hand left his shoulder holster, he was looking into the muzzles of the two long black guns that just "happened" in Slade's hands. It was his turn to look reflective.

"Never heard of but one feller I thought might be able to do it," he said. "Feller the Mexicans call E! Halcón—The Hawk. Folks say he's got the fastest gunhand in the whole Southwest. Reckon he has."

"Yes?" Slade smiled as he sheathed the big Colts.

"Yes!" Stiffy was emphatic.

"I've a notion," Slade observed, "that you can keep a tight *látigo* on your jaw."

"Guess you'll have to go a long ways to find a tighter," said Stiffy. "Let's have some more coffee."

After they had finished the coffee, Stiffy said, "I got a razor over there on the shelf if you'd care to mow off the whiskers. Got a notion you ain't a bad lookin' feller with that brush off your face."

"Thanks," Slade said. He had a shaving kit in his saddle pouches but accepted Stiffy's offer in the interest of his deception. That individual nodded approvingly after the stubble of beard was removed. When Francia arrived, in the late afternoon, she evidently noticed the change in his appearance, but the only remark she made was to again compliment him on the cleanliness of the place. Suddenly she turned to face him.

"I suppose you have a last name, Walt," she said. "What is it?"

Slade supplied it.

"Mine's Renshaw," she said.

"Francia Renshaw, a pretty name for a pretty girl," he observed.

"One that packs a whip!" she scoffed.

Abruptly, he smiled down at her from his great height. Reaching out, he gently plucked the whip from her shoulder, while she regarded him in wide-eyed surprise.

"See, it can be removed," he remarked pointedly.

"Yes," she replied, her voice low. "But please give it back. I feel naked without it."

Slade's eyes danced, but he did not make an obvious comment.

Perhaps she sensed what was passing through his mind, for she turned and hurried from the kitchen. Old Stiffy chuckled.

SIX

LATER, WHEN SLADE WAS BUSY at the lunch counter, Francia did comment on the change in his appearance, to Stiffy.

"What did I tell you?" she said. "He's positively handsome. But if you tell him I said so, I'll wear my whip out on you."

"Don't worry," Stiffy grinned, "I'll leave it to you to tell him."

"I won't!"

"Wanta bet?" said Stiffy, still grinning.

"Stiffy," she said, "although I couldn't think more of you if you were my father, there are times I'd like to shake you."

"Go ahead," Stiffy replied cheerfully, "I've been shook off by women before now."

Francia laughed, her little teeth flashing white against her red lips. Stiffy's grin became one of delight.

"The first real laugh I've heard you give since you came here," he said.

The emerald eyes grew pensive. " 'Just like the sun looking down at me from a blue sky,' " she repeated Stiffy's words of the night before. "Oh, the devil! I'm Francia, hard, vengeful woman with a whip!"

"Don't forget the red hair and the green eyes," Stiffy reminded her.

She shook her glowing curls and a dimple showed at the corner of her red mouth. Instantly, however, she was grave again. Her delicate black brows drew together.

"Stiffy, what is he?"

For once Stifffy was evasive with her; he felt she would quite likely learn the truth soon enough. Stiffy did *not* know that Walt Slade was a Texas Ranger.

"Hard to tell," he said. "His sort can be most anything."

"He speaks like an educated man."

"Wouldn't be surprised if he is," Stiffy agreed. "And he's a swamper in a saloon."

"Yes, a swamper in a saloon," Francia repeated slowly. "As out of place as an eagle in a barnyard."

Stiffy shot her a swift glance. He was struck by the aptness of the smile—an eagle, a hawk.

Francia sighed, and left the kitchen, Stiffy gazing after her. And his old eyes were compassionate.

A couple of uneventful days followed for Slade. While working, he carefully listened to conversations going at the bar and the table, but learned nothing of significance. He wondered if he was doing the wise thing by remaining where he was. And he began to grow decidedly restless.

Francia seemed to avoid him and he had very little direct intercourse with her. Which was not strange, however. The owner of a place doesn't usually mingle much with the swampers and the kitchen help. Every now and then, though, he would catch her eyes resting upon him, an inscrutable expression in their emerald depths.

She seldom showed up at the saloon before late afternoon or early evening, but on the fourth day she arrived before noon and approached Slade, who had arisen early and was giving Stiffy a hand in the kitchen.

"Walt," she said, "you don't like it here, do you?"

Slade straightened his back and gazed down at her. "It's not that I don't like it *here,*" he replied. "It's just that I happen to be more of a cowhand than a saloon swamper."

"I understand," the red-haired girl nodded. "If you're born to horse flesh and rope and branding iron, you never get them out of your blood. I was brought up on a ranch and I know. I'll tell you about that later, and there's something else I have to tell you. What I want you to do right now is get out of here for a while. Go take a long ride. That's what you need more than anything else. You'll find it interesting up the valley. Take your time and let the wind and the sunshine work on you for a while. Don't get back till after dark. This is a devil of a place on a sunny day; too many shadows. Get going."

34

She turned and left him before he could reply. He shrugged and headed for the stable. She was right, it would be good to get away for a while, in more ways than one. He wanted to look the section over and try and learn something about conditions in the valley from which cows had been wide-looped.

During the past days, Slade had visited Shadow from time to time.

"Don't you ever sleep?" the keeper had demanded querulously, on the occasion of his second visit. "I always find your bed not slept in."

"I'm pushing a mop in Francia's place and I've been sleeping there," Slade explained.

The keeper stared. "Sorta funny job for a cowhand," he commented.

"A man must eat," Slade replied, smilingly.

The keeper seemed to hesitate, then he said gruffly, "If you're sorta up against it, feller, never mind paying for the horse's keep; I like him."

Slade smiled down at the old fellow, and his cold eyes were very kind.

"Thank you," he said. "I appreciate that, greatly. Really, though, I'm able to pay for his keep, but thank you just the same." He patted the old man's shoulder and was rewarded by an embarrassed grin.

"Shadow," he remarked as they got under way, "Shadow, although we run up against some mighty ornery specimens in our business, just the same there are more good people in the world than bad ones. Let's go, horse!"

Twenty minutes later he was riding north across the prairie into the green and gold expanse of Tinaja Valley that rolled to the misty skyline, exulting in the glad sweep of the wind, the sunshine drenching the rangeland with molten bronze, the Autumnal glory of the hills.

He was not riding aimlessly; he had a definite objective in mind. He had gathered from Stiffy that Jackson Haynes, owner of the J Bar H, was just about the oldest inhabitant of the section; had been born here, and his father before him. Haynes should be familiar with conditions past and present. He felt he might be able to glean useful information from the rancher and had determined to pay him a visit. Stiffy had fairly well located Haynes's ranchhouse for him, so he rode north, trending somewhat east. And as he rode, he

35

studied the valley, which was geologically peculiar. On the east it was walled by a long line of perpendicular cliffs misty with distance. To all appearances they were unclimbable. To the west there were also cliffs, but their line was broken in places by long, gentle slopes that rose to a rounded skyline. Beyond those slopes and a shallow belt of hills, and to the north was New Mexico, where, Stiffy said, cattle rustled from the valley spreads were received by dealers in purloined stock. Could be.

Shortly before the death of his father, which occurred after financial reverses which occasioned the loss of the elder Slade's ranch, young Walt had graduated from a famous college of engineering. He had planned to take a post-graduate course in special subjects to better fit him for the profession of engineering. But at the moment there was no money for post-grads. While debating just what his next move would be, he was approached by Captain Jim McNelty, with whom he had worked some during summer vacations. Captain Jim had suggested that he come into the Rangers for a while and pursue his studies in spare time.

Slade thought the notion a good one, and in a way it was. Long since he had gotten more from private study than he could have hoped for from the post-grad.

But in the meanwhile, Ranger work had gotten a strong hold on him and he was loath to sever connections with the illustrious body of law enforcement officers. So he determined to stick with the Rangers for a while—he was young and there was plenty of time to be an engineer.

So at the moment he surveyed the valley with the eye of a geologist, and shrewdly suspected that a few million years before the valley and the desert to the southwest had been an arm of the sea. Some terrestrial convulsion had cut off the inlet and the water had, in the course of the ages, disappeared by evaporation. The valley, being of slightly higher elevation, caused the sea water to drain to the south leaving the valley floor fairly free of salt and other minerals. Vegetation had taken root and flourished in what was now the valley, while on the dessicated land to the south it had not. A not unusual formation, Slade had experienced others of a similar nature, but sometimes characterized by peculiar phenomena which were stumbled upon and then taken advantage of by the chance discoverer. A fact that Slade kept in mind.

He had covered quite a few miles and was approaching a long stretch of grove some five hundred yards ahead when, from beyond the grove, bulged a herd of cattle traveling at a great rate. Slade stared in astonishment.

"Now what loco coots are running the meat off the critters that way?" he wondered aloud to Shadow, who didn't have the answer or if he did refrained from saying so.

The herd streamed on, heading south by west. Another moment and horsemen appeared, urging the cows to greater speed. Slade knew they had sighted him, for he could see the white blurs of their faces turn in his direction.

From their ranks came a puff of smoke. An instant later a slug sang by overhead, fairly close. Another followed it, coming a mite closer.

Walt Salde didn't like to be shot at by total strangers, especially when to all appearances said strangers were in the act of perpetrating a crime. He signified his displeasure in unmistakeable terms and without delay. Whirling Shadow, he sent him racing back the way he had come. A hundred yards covered and he again whirled the tall horse to face the wide-loopers, for such he judged they were. Shadow stood perfectly motionless.

Sliding his heavy Winchester from the saddle boot, Slade clamped the butt to his shoulder; his eyes glanced along the sights and he squeezed the trigger.

Smoke puffed from the rifle muzzle. One of the riders whirled from his saddle as if struck by a giant fist. Slade could almost hear the shouts and curses as the others came skalleyhooting in his direction. Slugs whined past, but the back of a galloping horse is not a good shooting stance and none came very close.

"Terrapin brains!" he muttered, and squeezed the trigger.

A second man went down to lie still. Slade shifted the muzzle just a trifle, fired again and scored a miss because of the shifting of the target. He steadied the long gun and fired three shots in rapid succession. The result, a third empty saddle.

That was enough for the raiders. They turned their horses and sent them charging back toward the jostling herd. Slade followed, keeping his distance, and shooting. He saw a leg

37

fly up, but the rider, although he slumped forward, kept his seat. The demoralized rustlers swept past the herd and continued south by west. Slade slowed Shadow and approached the herd. He had no intention of pursuing the band. They knew the country and he didn't. He might easily run into a trap. He eyed their diminishing shapes warily, but they kept on going and soon dwindled from sight. Slade rode on to see what he had bagged. The blowing cows had halted and were regarding him apprehensively, rolling their eyes and rumbling. Slade's richly musical voice rose in a soothing melody as he dismounted beside the first body. The cows reacted as he expected them to and began to graze.

The dead man was an ordinary-appearing individual and his pockets discovered nothing of significance save a rather large sum of money, which the Ranger replaced. The same went for the other two. Rather salty-looking characters but in no way outstanding. The horses had galloped after the fleeing raiders, which he regretted, brands might have told something. Hardly likely, though. Apt to be Mexican skillet-of-snakes or unregistered burns and impossible to trace.

Rolling and lighting a cigarette, he straightened up and speculated the cows. All bore the J Bar H brand. Evidently Jackson Haynes's stock; he had passed a few clumps in the course of his ride.

"Guess we'd better take these perambulating beefsteaks home and let the folks there know what happened to them," he told Shadow. "Okay?"

Shadow offered no objections, so after a final glance to the southwest, although he had little fear that the raiders would return, he got the herd moving, shoving it almost due east toward where he figured the J Bar H casa should be.

SEVEN

SLADE'S ESTIMATE WAS SUBSTANTIALLY CORRECT and after about four miles of jogging he sighted a big white ranchhouse set in a grove. As he drew near he spotted a man sitting on the porch with his boots on the railing, and craning his neck in his direction. He appeared quite elderly and Slade surmised that he was Jackson Haynes himself. He kept the cattle moving until they were on the pasture that abutted the ranchhouse yard. Then he rode around the herd and to the veranda.

The man on the porch stared at him and brought his boots to the floor with a thump.

"Well, this is a new one!" he boomed. "Brought 'em here to show me how many you figure to swipe, eh? Say! what in blazes *is* the meaning of this?"

Slade dismounted and told him, tersely. The oldster exploded profanity. "And you did for three of the varmints? Fine chore! fine chore! Son, you're all right."

Several cowhands who had been occupied with chores around the barn and the blacksmith shop had desisted from their labors and were staring first at Slade and then at the cattle. The old man let out a whoop and one came running.

"Take the cayuse to the barn and give him everything he needs, the best," he ordered.

"Okay, Shadow," Slade said. The big black permitted himself to be led to the barn.

"One-man horse, eh?" commented the oldster. "I like that sort." He turned and ran his eye over the grazing herd.

"Nearly a hundred prime beef critters," he remarked. "Son, you've saved me a hefty passel of *dinero* today." He glanced at Slade's torn overalls and tattered shirt, thrust his hand into his pocket, glanced up at the sternly handsome face, withdrew the hand empty and held it out.

"Much obliged," he said. "My name's Haynes, Jackson Haynes. What's yours?"

Slade supplied it and they shook hands. "Come on in, come on in," invited Haynes. "Time for coffee and a snack. Come on in."

"Just a minute, sir," Slade said. "First I'd like for you to have a man ride to town and send a telegram to the sheriff of the county. He should come here and look things over."

"Guess you're right," nodded Haynes. He called to another cowboy who received his orders and hurried for his horse.

As they mounted the veranda steps, a girl appeared in the doorway. She was a tall girl and, Slade thought, rather pretty. Her hair was the color of ripe cornsilk, her eyes blue, her complexion very fair. She was dressed modishly, unusually so for the cow country, and her bearing was assured.

"Stella," said Haynes, "this young feller is Walt Slade, who just saved your old uncle a sizeable heap of money. Slade, my niece from New Orleans over Louisiana way, Stella Haynes."

"How are you, Mr. Slade?" the girl acknowledged, extending a shapely and very white hand, over which Slade bowed with courtly grace.

"I'll tell the cook to prepare something, Uncle Jack," she added and tripped back into the house.

"My brother's gal, here on a visit," Haynes volunteered as they entered the sumptuously furnished living room. "Sit down and make yourself comfortable. Snack be ready in a minute."

Slade occupied an easy chair, dropping his hat beside him and smoothing his thick black hair. Meanwhile he was studying Jackson Haynes and decided he liked him. A bluff old-timer who knew his way around and no doubt could be plenty salty did occasion warrant.

"So the hellions are at it again," Haynes growled as he stuffed black tobacco in a blacker pipe. "Thought maybe they'd trailed their twine. Been better'n a month since anybody hereabouts lost stock. Plenty lost before that. Maybe what happened today will sort of cool 'em down for a spell, don't you think?" Slade shook his head.

"I doubt it," he replied. "That sort isn't much affected by a setback; they'll be out to even the score, pronto." Old Jackson growled profanity.

"Where do you figure the cows go?" Slade asked. Haynes shrugged.

"Across to New Mexico, of course," he answered. "No place else for them to go."

"How about the Rio Grande and Mexico?"

"Across that desert?" Haynes scoffed. "No cows could do it without water, and there ain't no water on the Tinaja Desert." Slade nodded, and did not comment.

"You've trailed them to New Mexico?" he persisted. Haynes shook his head.

"We've trailed 'em and trailed 'em, with no luck," he said. "Over to the west of the cliffs and slopes and the hills is bar-

40

ren, rocky ground where hoofs won't leave a mark. There we always lose the trail, but it must turn north."

"The bunch I ran into today were headed south by slightly west," Slade observed.

"They'd turn north after they got across the slopes," Haynes declared positively. Slade did not argue.

Old Jackson regarded him speculatively. "New to this section, aren't you, son?" he said.

"I've passed through here a couple of times but never stopped off until this time," Slade replied, with truth.

"Who you working for now?"

"I'm pushing a mop in Francia's saloon in Olton," Slade replied. Old Jackson stared, and practically repeated the stablekeeper's words, "Funny sort of a job for a cowhand. Well, if you get tired of pushing a mop for Francia, there's a chore of riding all ready and waiting for you here. It's a good section to coil your twine in, even if we are pestered with cow thieves now and then."

"Thank you," Slade replied. "I'll keep it in mind."

"Francia?" said Stella from the door. "I've heard the boys talk about her. A good deal of a hoyden, is she not?"

"Depends on one's definition of a hoyden," Slade smilingly replied. Miss Haynes looked puzzled and went back to the kitchen. Old Jackson chuckled.

"Oh, I guess Francia's all right, even if she does run around half naked," he said. " 'Pears to know the cow business well as her brother did. He was okay, too, was Tom Renshaw. I felt mighty bad when I heard some devils had done him in. He was a good neighbor, and so is Francia, for that matter. All good neighbors hereabouts, and that counts for a heap. Up north the Whittaker brothers and the Carvels and the McPhersons are all prime folks. So is Sid Gholen over to the west. He's sorta new here. Came down from the Panhandle I believe about a year back, a little less I think. Bought the old Jensen place. It was pretty well run down and he got it cheap. Didn't take him long to put it in first class shape. Went right to work fixing things up. Brought in good stock and built the Swinging J into a going concern. Nice feller. A mite ringey and holds his comb a bit high, but he's all right. No, I can't complain about my neighbors. Even the new folks over west of the hills 'pear to be okay, though I don't know much about them. They moved in and took up

41

the State Land over there, a while after the railroad came through. Meet some of 'em in town now and then. Younger folks, most of 'em. We need the younger sort in this section—most of us are getting along and somebody'll have to take up where we leave off."

"The snack's on the table, Uncle Jack," Stella called from the doorway.

"About time," grunted Haynes. "My stomach's beginning to believe my throat's sewed up. Come along, son, I know you're hungry, too. Cowhands always are, or that's been my experience with them for the past sixty years or so. Come along."

The snack was bountiful and tastily prepared. Slade and old Jackson did it full justice. Stella sat with them, toying with her food. Slade noted that every time he glanced in her direction, her lashes fluttered down demurely and she would regard him through their silken fringe. She appeared to take no notice of his not at all presentable attire.

But she was pretty, he was forced to admit, and very feminine. He thought of Francia, her bare legs and her whip, and stifled a chuckle. Not much feminine about Francia, if one were to judge from outward appearances.

Later, when old Jackson had clumped out to see about something and they were alone in the living room, she, very adroitly, tried to induce him to talk about himself. Before long, however, she fell silent, appearing a little bewildered. Although she didn't know it, she was becoming conversant with a fact that had baffled wiser people. That Walt Slade would talk pleasantly, even volubly at times, but he wouldn't tell you anything. She compromised by talking about herself and her life in New Orleans, which Slade found interesting. And when he mounted his horse to head back to town, she said, "Come again—please do."

To which old Jackson added hearty assent.

EIGHT

As HE RODE through the scarlet and gold of the sunset, Slade reflected on the importance of seemingly trivial things. He had taken the job of a saloon swamper on impulse, with just the notion it would afford an excuse for sticking around the section for a while. But what he had learned of the killing of Tom Renshaw and Bates, the Rocking T range boss, confirmed definitely his belief that the outlaw bunch he was trailing might indeed have their headquarters somewhere in the section. Also, it might well provide him with the lead he needed.

"Anyhow, we made a start," he told Shadow. "Three isn't such a bad bag. Maybe the gents will be accommodating and give us another opportunity to get in a lick or two."

"Or collect a few," Shadow's snort seemed to say. Slade chuckled and rode on.

When he entered the saloon, Burk, the head bartender, beckoned him. There was a note of respect in the man's voice when he spoke.

"Miss Francia left early," he said. "I don't think she felt so good. She said for you to take charge tonight." He shot Slade a peculiar look and added, "she said for you to wear your guns."

Slade dissembled his surprise. "Okay," he said and went back to the kitchen. Old Stiffy greeted him with a grin.

"Well, how's the Big Boss?" he chuckled. "Liable to have your hands full, one way or another, before the night's over. It's payday for the spreads and the boys are all set to howl. Filling up fast already. First time I ever knew Francia to clear out on a payday night. Reckon she knows her business, though. Fact is I'm pretty sure she does."

"I hope so," Slade replied. He was still a bit surprised, and a trifle amused at his sudden and unexpected promotion. But never could tell what a redhead would do. Full of surprises as a barrel full of gophers.

43

"Have some coffee?" said Stiffy. "Something to eat whenever you want it."

Slade drank the coffee, then repaired to the saloon. Stiffy hadn't exaggerated, the place was filling up fast, with all the indications of a tumultuous night. He checked the games, saw that the bartenders were provided with everything needful and said a few words of caution to the dance-floor girls. He made sure that the dealers and the lookout were on the job.

It was past midnight and things were booming when Sid Gholen and Alf Crane, his range boss, entered. Both appeared to have pains in their tempers. They paused for a moment to speak with the head bartender. Slade saw them shoot glances in his direction, but he paid them no attention. They left the bar, found a vacant table and sat down. Their heads drew together in conversation. Gholen appeared to be urging something that Crane did not approve of. Finally, however, the range boss threw out his hands in a gesture of resignation and beckoned a waiter. Slade, with a multitude of things to look after, forgot all about them. A little later he had occasion to pass their table.

"Say, you," Gholen said abruptly, his voice arrogant, "this floor is a mess. Clean it up."

"All right, Mr. Gholen," Slade replied. "Have it taken care of immediately." He beckoned the man he had assigned to swamper duty for the evening. But Gholen was not satisfied.

"I told *you* to clean it up," he said. Looking for trouble, Slade instantly sensed, but he only replied, quietly, "Not this evening. I have other things to do."

Gholen leaned forward, his eyes narrowed. "Listen, fellow," he said, "when I tell you to do something, you do it. Remember what you got the last time you tangled with me."

Slade looked him up and down. "Don't try it again, Gholen," he said pleasantly. "You won't have near as much fun as you did the last time."

Gholen reddened with anger at the contempt in Slade's voice. Slade looked him squarely in the eyes, and laughed. Might as well get it over with.

With an oath, Gholen leaped to his feet, skirted the table and rushed, fists flailing. He met a sizzling left hook that

44

crashed him back against another table. He howled with anger, caught his balance and rushed again.

Slade had no intention of fooling with Gholen. He was big, pounds heavier than himself, and powerfully built. He met the rush with a straight right that sent the ranch owner reeling. Volleying oaths, Gholen came back for more, and got it. Another left hook rocked his head. A smash to the face staggered him. A right cross put his jaw in position and a straight left with all Slade's two hundred pounds behind it sent him to the floor. He stayed there.

Slade's eyes flickered to Alf Crane, who sat rigid, his hands beneath the table. He spoke three evenly spaced words, his voice quiet but fraught with deadly menace, "Don't—try—it!"

Crane didn't try it. Slowly and carefully he raised his hands and placed them palms down on the table top. Slade nodded approval and turned to find Stiffy beside him, his left hand gripping the left lapel of his coat.

"Just in case you didn't have an eye on Crane," he murmured through lips that did not move.

"Thanks," Slade replied.

"Not that I figured you'd really need me," Stiffy added. Slade smiled, beckoned a waiter and gestured to Gholen's prostrate form.

"Pour a glass of water over him and he'll come out of it," he said and turned to the jostling crowd.

"All right, folks," he called. "Back to your places. Entertainment's over. Get tickets from the lookout for the next show."

A roar of laughter greeted the sally. Order was restored. Admiring glances were bent on Slade.

"Fellow, you're good," chuckled Stiffy. "Plumb good!"

Gholen was reacting favorably to the water treatment. He sputtered, groaned, thrashed about and rolled over on his side. A moment later he sat up, looking dazed.

He was somewhat of a mess. Both eyes were blackening, his nose was swollen, his lips cut. He stared at Slade, unbelievingly, shook his head and got slowly to his feet. Then, unexpectedly, he grinned and stuck out his hand, almost repeating Stiffy's remark, "Feller, you're good. Hope there's no hard feelings. I'm not packing any."

Slade shook hands with him. Over Gholen's shoulder he

45

glimpsed Alf Crane's face. The range boss wore a look of cynical amusement. It appeared he was not exactly displeased at his boss's discomfiture. Perhaps because his advice had been disregarded.

"How about some coffee and a bite to eat?" Stiffy suggested. "You haven't had a thing and it's past midnight."

"Not a bad notion," Slade agreed. "Appears everything is under control for the moment."

"And I've a notion that after what happened to Gholen, everything will stay under control," Stiffy predicted.

In the kitchen, Stiffy remarked, "Well, looks like Gholen is man enough to pack a licking without holding a grudge."

"Yes, it *looks* that way," Slade replied dryly. Stiffy gurgled in his throat and poured a cup of coffee, his eyes snapping.

"What was the matter with Francia?" Slade asked as Stiffy placed a plate of food before him.

"Hanged if I know," Stiffy answered. "She came into the kitchen not long after you left and sat down and smoked a cigarette—she rolls 'em with one hand like a real puncher. All of a sudden she snapped out the butt and stood up.

" 'To the devil with this bad smelling, shadowy joint!' she said. 'I'm going out to the ranch. When Walt comes back, have Burk tell him to take charge of things tonight.' With that she was gone. Seemed all right except out of sorts. I wouldn't be surprised if she gets broody at times from thinking about her brother."

"Not beyond the realm of possibility," Slade conceded.

Stiffy proved himself a prophet with honor. The rest of the night passed without untoward incident. When Slade returned to the saloon, after eating, Gholen and Alf Crane were gone; they did not reappear.

Close to daylight, Slade went to bed and slept soundly. When he awoke and repaired to the kitchen, something after noon, Francia was already there.

"Hear you had yourself quite a night," she remarked. "Well, I guess Sid Gholen asked for it. He's a bit too quick on the trigger for his own good and everybody else's. He needed to be taken down a peg. Come on and we'll eat together. I haven't had any breakfast, either. Didn't feel like cooking for myself this morning and the cook hadn't gotten back from raising heck in town."

46

She led the way to an isolated table and they sat down opposite each other.

"Well, what did you do yesterday?" she asked.

"Among other things, I paid a visit to Jackson Haynes," Slade replied, mentioning no details. Francia regarded him, an inscrutable expression in her green eyes.

"How'd you like him?"

"Very much, a fine old jigger."

Francia was silent a moment, then, inconsequentially, "A girl there, isn't that so? I heard one was staying with him."

"Yes, his niece from New Orleans." Another hesitation. "Is she pretty?"

"Quite pretty," Slade replied, a smile twitching the corners of his mouth.

"And doesn't pack a whip?" The smile broadened.

"I doubt if she would know how to use one," he answered. "She's a city girl."

"Sophisticated and versed in all the wiles, I imagine." Slade's smile broadened still more.

"Really, I didn't notice," he replied. Miss Renshaw's expression plainly showed disbelief. Again she was silent for a moment. Abruptly she changed the subject.

"I said yesterday that I had something to tell you, something I wanted to talk to you about. First, though, did anything else happen in the course of your ride?"

Slade told her of his brush with the wide-loopers—she'd learn of it soon enough, anyhow. She listened in wide-eyed silence until he paused.

"Good heavens!" she breathed. "You might have been killed."

"Well, I wasn't," he returned cheerfully.

"Do you think it may cause you trouble with—the sheriff?"

"I doubt it," Slade replied, still cheerful. "I expect him to drop in some time this afternoon. He and I will have a little talk. Now what is it you wished to speak to me about?" Francia nodded.

"As I said, I was brought up on a ranch. But a few bad seasons plus wide-loopers caused Dad to lose his spread shortly before he died. I went to work in a bank, but I didn't like it. My brother drifted over this way and got into business and did well. I planned to come here and join him, sooner or later.

47

I figured to run the spread for him—I wasn't interested in the saloon."

"How'd you come to hang onto this place?" Slade asked, although he was pretty sure he already had the answer. "I understand you could sell without difficulty."

"There are a couple of reasons why," she explained. "First, the place is a money maker, and I need all I can get my hands on to pay off the mortgage on the ranch and to pay Sid Gholen the five thousand he lost when the place was held up and robbed."

"I don't think you have any legal obligation there," Slade commented.

"Perhaps not," she admitted, "but I consider there is an ethical obligation involved, which is even more important."

Slade nodded. He could understand that.

"But that is not my chief reason for hanging onto this place," she resumed. Her voice, usually so soft and rich, abruptly was harsh, her words evenly spaced.

"I've a feeling that the men who murdered my brother will come back here, sooner or later," she said. "I'm waiting."

"And if they do, you hope to even the score?"

"Yes."

Slade smiled, a little sadly. She was a competent and courageous woman, but pitted against such a bunch as murdered her brother and her range boss, she would have about as much chance as a rabbit in a houn'-dog's mouth.

"I suppose, too," she added, "that you've been wondering why I wear this outlandish costume. I'll tell you why—to attract attention. Men ride for miles just to get a look at me in it. They talk about it when they leave, and the word keeps getting farther and farther around. That's what I want —talk about me and talk about the place to get everywhere, down below the Mexican Border, into the hole-in-the-wall country to the southwest. When men talk about a woman and her affairs they are prone to exaggeration. Already plenty of people think this place is a gold mine instead of just a good money-maker as cowtown saloons go. I hope the right people hear it and get curious, and get notions. They might even consider the place worth another try like the last time. I'm waiting."

Slade regarded her in silence for a moment. The story intrigued him, and she intrigued him. It, he thought, denoted

48

imagination and a facile mind, and determination. However, he only said, "It's a hard trail to ride, the vengeance trail, with scant satisfaction at the end of it."

Francia's eyes flashed. "I think one is justified in avenging such a wrong," she said.

"Perhaps," he replied, "but still there thunders down through the ages, 'Vengeance is mine, sayeth the Lord. I will repay!' "

"But don't you think that God may use a human instrument with which to exact his vengeance?"

"Yes," Slade conceded, "but seldom indeed the one who is wronged. For then pride and hoped-for personal satisfaction are too strong. And God does not deal in vengeance, but in justice. Let Him choose His own instruments, for He will, no matter what we do or do not do."

The girl regarded him fixedly, and for the first time he saw uncertainty in the emerald eyes.

"Perhaps you are right," she sighed. "I never thought of it in just that light. Now I have something more cheerful to talk about."

"Yes?"

"Yes. As I said yesterday, you are not satisfied here, and I don't expect you to be. I kept you on these days because I wanted to study you and learn if you are what I wanted. I have decided you are. As Stiffy told you, my range boss, who was with my brother before me, was killed last month. It left me on considerable of a spot. I have nearly a dozen hands riding for me. They are tops at range work, but that is as far as they go. I need somebody to keep an eye on them and run the spread as it should be run. I can't do it myself with this infernal joint on my hands. I haven't the time to study problems, solve them and make decisions. As you have probably heard, we are being stolen blind, or were, up to something over a month back. Now I've a good notion it is going to start again. Nobody seems to know how it is being done. If I had the time to devote to it, perhpas I could find out. But I haven't. I'm badly in need of a competent range boss, a manager, rather, to take charge of the ranch and run it as it should be run. I feel you can do it, so I'm offering you a job as range boss on the Rocking T. What do you say?"

Slade reflected a moment. He had a feeling that in some

49

way the Rocking T would be the focus of the outlaw activities in the section. He had come to the conclusion that there was little to be learned in the saloon and was indeed about ready to resign his position, if position it could be called. He arrived at a decision, with reservations.

"All right," he said, "on the condition that I am to handle things as I think best, without interference by the owner or anybody else."

It was Francia's turn to hesitate. Then she too appeared to make up her mind.

"Okay," she said. "We'll let it go at that." She held out her hand and they shook to seal the bargain, like two men. Slade's lips quirked a trifle at the corners.

"Excuse me a minute," said Francia. She arose and passed behind the bar, returning a few minutes later with a handful of money which she shoved at Slade.

"Here," she said. "Here's your pay for your work here, and a month's advance wages. I'll take it out at the rate of ten dollars a month till it's paid up. Go buy yourself some decent clothes. I don't want my range boss looking like a chuck-line tramp."

Slade took the money, carefully divided it into two unequal sums, the larger of which he shoved back to Francia.

"This," he said, "is the pay for my work here. It will be sufficient for my needs. I'll draw my pay as range boss after I've earned it."

The red hair seemed to crackle. "Mr. Slade," she snapped, "I'm accustomed to having the people who work for me do as I say."

"So I assume," Slade replied. "But there's always a time to call a halt. This is it."

For a moment she glared at him. Then suddenly a wave of color mantled her creamily tanned cheeks. Her long lashes fluttered down, not in invitation as had done those of Stella Haynes, but to hide what might be read in her eyes.

"Very well," she said, her voice low and very soft.

NINE

HAD NOT FRANCIA AND STIFFY both been pledged to silence, they might have compared notes. In which case, some misunderstandings would have been cleared up and probably some difficulties avoided.

A few days before, Slade had met the Mexican day swamper on the floor. The old fellow stared, then bowed his head reverently, as to a shrine. Slade smiled and shook his head the merest trifle. The swamper nodded his understanding. Slade spoke a few words in Spanish that caused his wrinkled face to glow with pleasure, and passed on.

Sharp-eyed Francia had noted the bit of byplay. A little later she cornered the swamper.

"Miguel," she said, "you seem to know him."

"*Si?*"

"Yes, Mr. Slade. Miguel, who is he, and what is he?"

The old man hesitated, his eyes fixed on her face. What he read there, perhaps, caused him to smile in a pleased manner.

"*Patrona,*" he replied, "what the ears hear the heart will keep to itself alone?"

"Yes."

"He is El Halcón."

"El Halcón?" Francia repeated. "Seems to me I have heard that name before."

"Doubtless you have, and will again," said Miguel. Mission taught, he continued in the flowery idiom of *Méjico,* "He is El Halcón, the just, the compassionate, the friend of the lowly. The friend and champion of all who know wrong or sorrow or oppression. There are those who say that he is evil, but they are either evil themselves or do not understand. He is a strange man. Out of the nowhere he comes, into the nowhere he goes. He walks the earth as did Our Lord in the days of old, in honor, kindliness and clean mirth. Among the lowly he has many friends; also among those who

51

sit in the seats of the mighty. Where is El Halcón, evil cannot abide, and when he departs evil has already departed, leaving peace, happiness, and freedom from fear. *Patrona,* you will learn."

"*Gracias,*" Francia said and walked away, a pucker between her black brows.

While Slade and Francia were still talking at the table, three men entered. The foremost was a tall and lean individual with a leathery countenance and a drooping gray mustache. A big nickel badge was pinned to his shirt front. He was Sheriff Rolf Harty and the others were two of his deputies. He spoke a word to the deputies and they ambled to the bar. The sheriff glanced around, spotted Francia and sauntered to the table.

"Howdy, Francia?" he said. "I'm looking for a gent named Slade."

"Guess you've found him, Sheriff," Francia replied, gesturing to her table companion. She performed the introductions and the two men shook hands solemnly.

Francia stood up. "I'll leave you gentlemen," she said. "No doubt you have things to talk about." She glanced at Slade, whose eyes were dancing, and again the color rose in her cheeks.

"I'll send over a drink," she said hurriedly and headed for the bar. The sheriff chuckled.

"How are you, Walt?" he said as he sat down. "And how's McNelty?"

"Fine as frog hair," Slade replied. "He told me to say hello for him if I happened to contact you, which he thought likely I would."

"He thought right," grunted Harty. "When you show up in a section, peace officers begin jumping through hoops. Suppose he sent you to round up that bunch of hellions that have been raising the devil all the way from Brownsville? Learn anything?"

"Enough to cause me to believe that their headquarters is somewhere hereabouts," Slade answered.

"Wouldn't be surprised," nodded Harty. "This is a prime section for such scalawags to hole up. Now I've got something to tell you. Old Jackson Haynes and some of his boys steered me to where you told them the bodies would be found. We found plenty of blood splashes, and the grass was beaten down where they'd laid for quite a while, but we didn't find any bodies. What do you think about that?"

"I think it corroborates my opinion that their hangout *is* somewhere in this section," Slade answered. "They apparently didn't desire that those bodies be placed on exhibition."

"My sentiments," said the sheriff. He glanced at Slade's disreputable clothing and chuckled again.

"Haynes told me you've taken up swamping as a profession," he observed. "Well, right now you look it."

"Nope," Slade smiled. "I'm range boss for the Rocking T."

"The devil you are! Getting up in the world, eh? Well, you always did have a way with women, but I've a notion that this time you'll find your hands full. She's a hellcat for fair."

"At least she strikes a good pose," Slade conceded.

The sheriff grunted derisively. "Not but what they all ain't. Sometimes I think I like the Francia kind best—less liable to stick a knife in your back when you ain't looking," said the confirmed bachelor of fifty-seven. "Here she comes now. Darned good looking, all right; but red hair and green eyes! Gentlemen, hush!"

Francia appeared to be again her composed self. "I've a notion you could stand something to eat, Sheriff," she said. "Your boys, too, if you can get them away from the bar. Give the waiter your orders—everything on the house. Walt, come out to the kitchen, please, I have something to show you."

When they reached the kitchen, Slade asked, "What have you to show me?"

"Nothing," Francia replied. "That was just to get you away. I wanted to know how you made out with him?"

"Why, fine," Slade replied in surprise. "He's a good old jigger. What made you think I wouldn't?"

"Well, I—I—oh, blast it! Can't a girl worry?"

She flounced back into the saloon. Slade stared after her, shook his head and returned to the sheriff.

Harty pushed back his empty plate with a sigh of content and hauled out his pipe.

"Anyhow, even if she *is* a hellcat, she's all right," he said. "Yep, a real gal. Well, I see the boys have finished eating, too, so I'm heading back to town—be after dark when we get

53

there, as it is. If you want anything, just let me know. Good luck to you, and remember me to old Jim."

After the sheriff departed, Francia came over to the table.

"I think you'd better hustle out and buy those clothes before the stores close," she said. "We've got things to do. Looks like we're going to have another busy night."

Slade did buy a shirt and overalls, to replace the garments he discarded as useless, leaving his change, which he would need sooner or later, in his saddle pouches. Then he paid Shadow a visit and found him in a fairly good temper.

"I'll hang onto the stall and the room," he told the stable-keeper, after informing him of his promotion to range boss. "I expect to be in town every now and then and will want a place to squat."

"Okay," agreed the keeper. "Sorry to see you leave—I'll miss the horse. Glad you're doing all right, though; you weren't made for mopping a saloon."

Francia was right when she prophesied another busy night. By soon after dark the place was roaring. Around midnight, Sid Gholen came in, alone, and occupied a table. He had quite a few souvenirs to show for the ruckus the night before. Both eyes were discolored, his nose still swollen, a purple lump on the side of his jaw. When he sat down he did it gingerly and winced. Doubtless his ribs were sore. However, he waved to Slade cordially and smiled. Slade waved back, but it seemed to him that the smile on Gholen's lips never reached his eyes.

Francia paused beside Slade, glanced over his new attire again and again nodded approval.

"Clothes may not make the man, but they sure make a difference in his appearance," she said.

Slade smiled and glanced down. Francia made a face at him.

A little later, Alf Crane came hurrying in. Slade thought he was laboring under suppressed excitement. He sat down beside Gholen and their heads drew together. Slade would have been highly interested could he have heard the conversation that followed.

"Sid," the range boss said, "do you want to know who that big hellion is?"

"Sure, who is he?" replied Gholen.

"I was in a rumhole down the street," Crane said. "There

were some Mexicans talking together there and I listened. Sid, that ice-eyed devil is El Halcón!"

"What!"

"That's right, El Halcón, the smartest and saltiest owlhoot in Texas." Gholen muttered profanely.

"And you had to tangle with him," Crane added in exasperated tones. "It's a wonder he didn't kill you. Figured to impress the gal by handing him a larrupin'. You wouldn't have impressed her; you would have just made her hate you. I saw her that first night you hit him. Her eyes were like a mad cat's. I thought she was going to wear that whip out on you."

"If she'd tried it, I'd have taken it away from her and cut her to ribbons with it," Gholen said, his voice a vicious snarl.

"Uh-huh, and then that lookout with the sawed-off and half a dozen other gents in here would have *blown* you to ribbons. Don't lay a hand on a good woman in this section, Gholen. Do it and you'll sign your death warrant. You ain't down below the line, now."

Gholen subsided to mutterings under his breath.

"I wonder what El Halcón wants here?" he demanded querulously, a moment later.

"I don't know, but whatever it is it'll mean trouble for somebody," predicted Crane.

"What are we going to do about him?"

"Get him out of the way, if we can," Crane replied. "It'll have to be done mighty smart, though; he's poison. I'll think on it. You won't have much chance tieing onto the Rocking T as you plan to, even though you do figure to buy up the mortgage with the money we—with the money you've got."

"Yes, he'll have to be gotten rid of, but how?" said Gholen.

The glitter in Crane's black eyes became more pronounced. "I'll think on it," he repeated.

The night, though rough and rowdy and tumultuous, passed without serious incident. It was almost daylight when Slade and Francia set out for the Rocking T ranchhouse.

Slade glanced at his companion. She did not look at all like a hellcat right now; she looked like a pathetic and very weary small girl. She interpreted his glance and smiled wanly.

"I am tired, terribly tired," she admitted. "I feel as if I could hardly stay in the saddle."

"We'll take care of that," Slade said. He reached out, plucked her from the hull and held her in front of him, close. She stared at him in bewilderment. Then the dimple showed at the corner of her mouth and she snuggled closer.

"This is better," she sighed. "I actually believe I can go to sleep."

"Do so," Slade said. He spoke to Shadow and the great black smoothed his pace, Francia's mount ambling along beside him. When Slade glanced down at the girl, her black lashes were shadows against her cheeks and her red lips were slightly parted. She *was* sound asleep.

The false dawn was flitting ghost-like across the sky when they reached the Rocking T ranchhouse, a small but tightly built structure set advantageously in a grove of ancient piñons and near the trail.

Francia opened her eyes and smiled drowsily as he pulled up at the veranda steps. He dismounted lithely, with her still in his arms, and carried her up the steps and into the house.

The plainly furnished living room was something of a contrast to the sumptuous J Bar H, but it was clean, comfortable and orderly. Looking somewhat out of place in its surroundings was a massive grand piano.

"I'll take care of the horses, you go to bed," he told her as he set her on her feet.

"I feel fine now," she said. "Don't remember when I slept so well. I'm going to make us some coffee."

"Okay, wouldn't go bad right now," Slade agreed. "I'm going to bed down the cayuses."

"A lantern hanging just inside the barn door," Francia said. "Don't worry about the boys. I told them you were riding with me tonight, so they won't be bothered."

After taking care of the horses, Slade returned to the house, where he found the coffee nearly ready. Francia had found time to change to a robe, golden in color, that clung closely to the ripe curves of her form. Her smoldering hair was brushed back softly from her white forehead.

"This better than short pants or Levi's?" she asked. "Oh, I like to feel like a woman now and then, instead of a freak. Sit down, the coffee's ready now."

"I don't think you could conceal your womanliness in a

56

blanket," Slade said with a smile and was rewarded with the dimple.

They drank the coffee mostly in silence, for Francia was still tired, and so was Slade. She rinsed the cups and said, "I'll show you where you'll sleep."

They mounted the stairs. Francia paused at a door midway down the hall. Opening it, she touched a match to a bracket lamp and the soft glow showed a comfortably furnished room with two windows.

"It was Bates's," she said. "I like to have my range boss within call, in case I should need him. The cook sleeps in the bunkhouse and there isn't any room to spare there. I sleep in the room at the head of the stairs, and if you happen to need me for any reason, don't hesitate to call."

"I won't," Slade promised, smiling.

"And now I'll show you something else," she said, "a real bathroom. There is a tank on the roof supplied with water from a spring by a hydraulic ram. See, there's even a shower."

"Just like city folks," Slade chuckled.

"Yes," she nodded. "Tom had advanced notions. Now I'm going to bed, and you'd better, too. Sleep late and then you'll meet the boys and take charge."

TEN

SLADE DID SLEEP LATE, and when he descended to the living room, he found Francia there, in shirt and overalls.

"Remember, I slept the whole twelve miles from town to the *casa*," she reminded him when he remarked on her early rising. "We'll have breakfast together and then I'll have to be riding. Have a lot to do at the saloon today. I told the boys to all be here by two o'clock, so you can meet them."

They ate a leisurely breakfast and then Slade watched her ride away, swaying lithely to the movements of her horse.

The cook, a rotund and cheerful individual, brought him

coffee in the living room and he relaxed with a cigarette until the hands filed in.

Most of the Rocking T hands were young punchers, a happy-go-lucky, carefree lot. Slade recalled seeing several of them in the saloon on payday night, but at the time he did not know they were Francia's riders.

One, however, was a gray-haired, wrinkled old waddie named Sime Collins, who had been with the spread before the days of Tom Renshaw's ownership. Slade singled him out as the best source of information relative to conditions and what had been going on. He asked about the rash of rustling that had broken out in the past six months.

"They were stealing us blind up to about a month ago," Collins declared. "Then all of a sudden it stopped; but I heard about what happened on the J Bar H the other day— you did a good chore—and I figure they're likely to bust loose again, now. Of course we weren't by ourselves—all the spreads were catching it—but fellers like Haynes and Gholen can take it, for a while. A small outfit like this one can't. Even without mortgage payments to be met it couldn't. There's a smart bunch of devils operating in the section. The spreads over to the west of the valley have been losing some, too, or so they say, but not so much as outfits over here."

"And you figure they are run to New Mexico?" Slade asked.

"Where else could they be run?" Collins countered. "The stock here is improved stuff and sorta heavy. Maybe the longhorns over to the west might make it across the desert to Mexico without water, though I wouldn't want to bet on it, but not our kind of critters."

"And you've never been able to trail them to New Mexico?"

"Never have," Collins admitted. "Always lose tracks on the bad land just west of the hills."

"I see," Slade said thoughtfully and let the subject drop. "You and I will take a ride together," he said. "The rest of you boys can get back to your chores. I'll have another talk with you in the morning."

Until dusk, Slade and the old waddie rode over the range, Collins pointing out salient features, Slade asking questions which Collins, thoroughly versed in his business, had no difficulty answering.

It took but one more day of riding to cause Slade to come to the conclusion that the spread was a good one but was far from being made the most of.

"This place making money?" he asked Francia before she started on her ride to town.

"If it wasn't for the thieving we would just about break even," she replied.

"There's no good reason why you shouldn't do a bit better than break even," Slade told her. "In the first place you are using too much range for the number of cows you've got and the number of hands to look after them. They should be herded more to the north where the grass and water are better and not allowed to scatter all over the place. That's not much of a chore with your kind of cows. They're heavier than longhorns and not so much the roving type. Cows like to hole up in those stony and brush-grown gulches to the south, but they don't put on weight properly there, and calves die in those hole-ups or get grabbed off by coyotes and wolves.

"And don't forget, those south pastures are made to order for cow thieves. Easy for even brush-popping owlhoots to run off a few head any dark night, to say nothing of the smart and salty outfit it appears is operating in this section. You'd have to have ten times your number of hands to properly patrol such a terrain. While with only the north pastures in use, your bunch can keep an eye on things with little difficulty.

"Where the wide-loopers take the cows after they cut them out I don't as yet know, but there's no sense in making it easy for them. And another disadvantage of having the critters down on those south pastures. Your brand is an easy one to alter. Some unscrupulous outfit in the section you'd never suspect may be doing a bit of brand blotting. And there are other things I won't bother you with right now.

"But don't worry, all that is going to be changed, pronto."

Looking at him, Francia had no doubt but that it would.

The following morning, Slade issued his powders tersely and to the point.

"Now you know what I want done, so go ahead and do it,"

59

he concluded. "Collins, you take charge for a while; I'll see you later."

"Wonder where he's going?" one of the younger hands asked as Slade rode off, south by west.

"Hard to tell," replied Collins. "Maybe to some hilltop where he can watch and see if we're loafing on the job,"

"Well, he ain't going to catch me loafing on the job," the puncher declared, with emphasis. "I was in the saloon the night he gave Sid Gholen that workout, and Gholen is supposed to be a raunchin' good man with his fists. I'd sooner tangle with a mountain lion and give him first holt."

"Yep, he's salty, all right," said Collins. "But, I betcha, a man to ride the river with."

There was universal agreement to the high compliment.

Slade did not ride to a hilltop from which he could observe what went on in the valley. Instead, he rode steadily south by slightly west until he figured he was about opposite where he had the run-in with the wide-loopers. Then he turned west and sent Shadow up a long and gentle slope. On the crest he pulled up to give the horse a breather and gazed back the way he had come.

From the elevation, the valley lay before him like a map, one of those unexpected formations of the Trans-Pecos region that burst on the eye of the wanderer like a mirage. Typical of this grim and austere land that nevertheless was always ready to give bountifully to those who dared its fastnesses and its threat.

Slade rode across the crest and again pulled up to gaze to where the mountains of New Mexico were but a blue pencil line against the sky. Then he turned and gazed south by west toward the arid expanse of the desert, beyond which was the Rio Grande and Mexico. He rolled a cigarette, smoked it and then sent Shadow down the western slope at the low hills.

Here, as he had been told, the land was stony, baked by the sun and scantily grown with occasional tufts of grass. The condition prevailed for several miles before it gave place to the verdant grassland. Here, unexpectedly, the slope of the land was from west to east, which explained the semi-desert that shouldered the base of the hills. He rode onto the inhospitable expanse for a mile or so, scanning the ground the while and coming to the conclusion that it would be well nigh impossible, even for the eyes of El Halcón, to discern signs of passing cattle. He turned Shadow's head and rode south.

Now he rode very slowly in long zig-zags, quartering the ground which he studied with the greatest care. From time to time he would raise his eyes to gaze south toward the slowly nearing desert. Then again toward the shadowy uplift of the New Mexico hills and mountains, estimating distances, trying to vision possible routes.

Eventually he found what he sought, the indubitable evidence that cattle in large numbers had passed that way, heading south by west. After a while he pulled up and rolled another cigarette.

"Shadow," he said, "I was right. They do go south to the desert. How do they cross it without water on the way? That one I can't answer just yet, but I intend to find the answer before the last brand is run. Horse, I think some folks in this section are in for one devil of a surprise."

Why had nobody else learned that the cows really had gone south instead of west? Slade felt the answer to that was simple enough. The section was convinced that the desert could not be crossed by purloined cattle, so no thought was given to a possible southern route, and pursuit centered invariably on the country between the valley and the New Mexico State Line. A continually futile pursuit, for the cows didn't go that way.

The second answer was that the inhabitants of the section were cattlemen and while able enough in their own field, they lacked the intensive training to which the Texas Rangers were subjected. And, incidentally, for the most part at least, they lacked El Halcón's keen mind and his meticulous attention to detail. And few indeed had El Halcón's abnormally keen eyesight.

Which was all very well, but so far El Halcón hadn't the slightest notion as to how the cows were gotten across the burning desert without water.

He continued his ride, finding more signs of the passage of cattle, not at all to his surprise. Finally he reached the edge of the desert and sat gazing across its arid expanse of sand, salt, and alkali.

It was small, as deserts went in this land of great distances, but it was deadly, especially when the sudden storms swept across it, raising the sand in blinding clouds, as Slade had good reason to know. Even a horseman was taking chances when he ventured onto the inhospitable terrain. To drive a herd across the full forty miles of desolation, even traveling mostly at night, seemed sheer nonsense and a good way to find a grave for both cows and riders.

But evidently it could be done, and if he hoped to break up the practice, and incidentally, he was convinced, drop a loop on the elusive band of robbers and killers, he must learn how it was done.

"Not today, though," he told Shadow. "When we make a try we'll endeavor to traverse the first twenty miles or so at night. If there is water out there somewhere, it must be about half way across. Well, we'll see. Now suppose we amble back to the valley and see how the boys are making out with their chores. Got to do something to earn our keep, so far as the Rocking T and its pretty red-headed owner is concerned."

Slade took his time on the homeward ride, for he felt confident old Sime Collins would have everything under control.

"He'll make her a good range boss after we trail our twine," he remarked to Shadow.

"Uh-huh, *after*," Shadow's snort seemed to say.

"Now don't get notions in your *loco* head," Slade warned. "You heard what I said."

Shadow did not appear impressed and ambled on sedately.

When Slade arrived at the valley, he found the work progressing in a satisfactory manner, and when the hands rode in to supper he complimented them.

"And it'll make it easier for you boys," he told them. "A much easier range to work."

"You're darned right," growled Collins. "I lost two shirts in those blankety-blank mesquite-choked gulches to the south. We'll have 'em all rooted out and druv north in a few more days."

"It should have been done long ago," Slade observed.

"Uh-huh, but Bates, a mighty good man with a horse and a rope, was sorta oldfashioned, I reckon. Also, he wasn't used to this kind of range. Came from the Panhandle country where I gather a man can stretch his legs. And Tom Renshaw hadn't got things really going before he was killed. Besides, that blankety-blank-blank saloon kept him busy. About all he managed to get done on the spread was to build the *casa* over and make a lot of improvements. Reckon he'd have straightened the spread out if he'd ever got time."

Slade nodded his understanding. He knew the Bates kind, men used to the vast ranches of the north and east which, for all their tremendous acreage were easy to work. Different in the Trans-Pecos country where there were degrees of difficulty and where the shrewd cowman took advantage of his best land and fought shy of the terrain in which the cows liked to hole up; it was a hefty chore to root them out.

Slade had seen very little of Francia during the busy days, but the second evening she was waiting for him when he rode in.

"Walt," she said, "I've been thinking over what you told me about my brand. I think I will have it changed."

"A good idea," Slade agreed.

"Have you any suggestions?"

"Well, an F Lazy R would be much harder to slick-iron," he replied. "A really good rewrite man can alter most any brand, but there aren't too many of that sort around, fortunately."

"All right," Francia decided. "I'll do it. And here is a list of stores the cook says he needs to have sent out. I'm going to sleep in a room over the saloon tonight. Suppose you meet me at noon tomorrow and we'll attend to the registration of the brand and the other chores. So long, I've got to be riding; I'm late already."

Noon of the following day found Slade in Olton. He stabled his horse and walked to the saloon. Francia was in front of it, and she was in a thoroughly bad temper.

"Walt," she greeted him, "I think I made a mistake when I took you off the swamper job and made you a range boss."

"Wouldn't be surprised," Slade agreed cheerfully, "but why?"

"Because you were the only swamper, aside from Miguel, I ever had I could depend on. Last night the one I hired went off and got drunk and I haven't seen hide or hair of him since. And to make matters worse, Miguel has a bad cold and didn't come in today; I told him not to. Nobody to help Stiffy in the kitchen, nobody to keep the barroom looking decent. The Rafter K and the Tree L shipping herds rolled in this morning. The bar's packed and we had forty dinners to serve. I've worked myself blind. I'm a mess and I haven't had time to change and clean up."

Looking her over, Slade was inclined to agree, although he thought that she was a decidedly delectable "mess." Her Levi's were dusty and streaked and there was a grease spot about the size of a dinner plate across the front of her silk shirt. Her red hair was flying wildly and there was a smudge across her nose. She rubbed said nose vigorously and the smudge spread to one sun-golden, rose-tinted cheek. Slade had to grin.

Which, not unnaturally, did not tend to improve Miss Renshaw's temper; but there was worse to come. Just as she glared at him and started to speak her mind in no uncertain terms, there was a grinding of wheels and a trim buckboard paused at the edge of the board sidewalk. In it were Jackson Haynes and his niece.

Stella wore some sort of faultless creation of pale blue. A cocky little hat perched on the side of her yellow curls which were in perfect order. She looked cool, dainty and exquisite. She waved her slender white hand and shrilled a greeting to Slade.

"Walt!" she called reproachfully, "you promised you'd come again and you never have. Please do."

"Yep, show up some time, son," old Jackson added cordially.

"Please do," Stella repeated.

"Thank you," Slade said, without committing himself. He glanced at Francia, whose face was utterly expressionless. His glance swung back to the vision of loveliness in the buckboard and mirrored the approval that was due her. He glanced again at the dusty, dishevelled and besmudged Francia, his eyes mirthful. Any woman worth her salt, and Miss Renshaw was worth more than a shakerful, would have correctly interpreted that glance of comparison. But Francia's expression was still inscrutable save for a reddish glint in her green eyes.

The buckboard rolled on, Stella shrilling a goodbye. Slade turned to Francia.

"Well, all set to take care of those chores?" he asked.

But the unpredictable redhead had a surprise in store for him.

"You take care of them," she replied. "I'm going home. Tell Burk to take charge of the place tonight." She turned on her heel and marched into the saloon.

Slade handled the chores. There was a wagonload of stuff needed for the spread. Followed a lengthy discussion anent the new branding irons, the storekeeper promising to take care of the registration, which involved filling out complicated forms. It was late when Slade ate his dinner in the kitchen of the saloon and had a talk with Stiffy, and well past dark when he reached the ranchhouse.

After taking care of his horse, he walked to the ranchhouse. As he drew near he heard somebody playing the piano, rather nicely he thought, and singing in a low but sweet contralto voice. Opening the door, he stepped into the living room, and stared.

ELEVEN

FRANCIA WAS SEATED AT THE PIANO. She wore a dress of flame colored silk, cut very low, that clung to every singing line of her lithe young form. Her hair, smoldering in the lamplight, was exquisitely arranged, more vivid than her dress. Her neck and shoulders rising from the glowing fabric were foam-white. Slade wondered if there was another redhaired woman in the world who would dare wear a dress of that color. She turned her head, smiled at him and went on singing.

Slade sat down in his favorite chair and rolled a cigarette. Abruptly, Francia stopped singing and playing and turned to face him.

"Well," she said, "do you like me better this way?"

"This way?" he repeated in simulated surprise. "Oh, I see, you're wearing a dress."

Francia glared at him. "I think," she said, "that you are the most exasperating person in the world." She gave the keys an angry thump that jangled discords from the piano.

65

"Why?" he asked mildly. "I thought your playing and singing were not bad."

"Do you think you could improve on them?" she said.

"Possibly," he replied.

Francia whisked off the stool. "All right, let's hear you try," she snapped.

With a smile, Slade crossed to the piano, adjusted the height of the stool and sat down. Francia's eyes widened as he ran his fingers over the keys with a master's touch. For a moment he played a beautiful and haunting melody, then he threw back his black head and sang.

And as his great golden baritone-bass pealed and thundered through the room, his listener sat entranced, eyes wide, lips slightly parted.

The music ended in a crash of chords. Slade turned to her, smiling.

"Yes," she said slowly, "you undoubtedly are the most exasperating person in the world. "With all the refinements of cruelty at your fingertips. Why didn't you tell me you could play and sing like that?"

The singingest man in the whole Southwest stood up. He walked to the chair, leaned over and kissed her lightly. For an instant her lips clung to his, then she drew back, one hand pressed against her mouth.

"Why did you do it?" she breathed. "You shouldn't have done it. I'm a dedicated woman. Dedicated to—"

"That's enough," he told her sternly. "We went over all that the other night. I don't want to hear any more of it."

"But I tell you—"

"Shut up!" he interrupted. "Tighten the *látigo* on your jaw. You talk too much."

She gazed at him for a moment, then, as most any normal woman would have done under the circumstances, she began to cry. Which had much more effect on Slade than a tantrum would have had.

He picked her up, sat down and cradled her in his arms, even as he had done that first night they rode to the ranch together. She sobbed against his shirt front.

Suddenly she raised her head and regarded him through her tears. "I was so lonely," she breathed. "But I'm not any more, and I won't be—for a while."

"A while?"

66

"Oh, you won't stay. Your kind never stays. But it'll be nice to have you while you're here. I'll make the most of you while I've got you."

"Yes?"

"Yes."

They blew out the light and ascended the stairs together.

Slade and Francia ate breakfast with the hands the following morning. Francia's eyes were downcast and when they met Slade's glance, the color in her cheeks deepened. Nobody paid any attention, however, for the punchers were busy with their food and discussion of the day's chores.

As Slade was heading for the barn to get the rig on Shadow, Francia whispered, "Dear, come back in the early afternoon and ride to town with me. Please."

"Okay," he agreed. "I guess Sime can look after things."

"I'm sure he can," Francia said. "I'll be waiting for you."

They rode to Olton through the golden afternoon sunshine, their mounts close together. When they reached the town, Francia insisted on accompanying him to the stable to put up the horses.

"I don't want you to get out of my sight," she explained, smiling and dimpling at him.

With the cayuses cared for, they walked to the saloon. Francia was just entering when two men stepped from a doorway a few paces down the street. One was a tall, lean, saturnine-looking individual with a cast in one eye. The other was blocky, red-faced and bearded. As they stepped into view, they fanned out.

"El Halcón!" the red-faced man shouted. "The sheriff wants him!" Both went for their guns. The street seemed to explode to the bellow of reports.

Walt Slade, blood trickling from the fingers of his left hand, peered through the smoke fog at the two forms on the ground. The red-faced man lay on his back, dead. The other writhed and retched with a bullet-smashed shoulder. Slade eyed him closely, but he was too shocked and shaken to be dangerous any longer. The Ranger turned to meet Francia, who was running to him, gasping and sobbing.

"Oh, darling, you're hurt!" she cried. "You're hurt!"

67

"Nothing to it—slug nicked my arm," he said, holstering his Colts and patting her shoulders soothingly. "Take it easy a minute, now."

Men were boiling from doors, grouping around the downed gunmen.

"Hey! I know these devils!" shouted a lank old frontiersman. "This one still kicking is Slow Baker. The other hellion is Shotgun Blue. Find the town marshal, somebody. He'll be glad to see old Slow. Understand there's a reward notice out for *him*."

"What about El Halcón, if the tall feller *is* El Halcón?" somebody cried. "They said the sheriff wants *him*."

"Sheriff wants El Halcón, the devil!" snorted the frontiersman. "No sheriff ever wants *him*. Didn't you see how chummy Sheriff Harty was with him the other day. Use your head!"

He strode to Slade and stuck out his hand. "Shake, feller," he said. "You did a fine chore. Those two hellions are hired guns. Nobody's ever been able to pin anything on them, but they should have stretched rope long ago. They were out to get you. I don't know why, but they were. And I betcha some son of a skunk hired them to do the chore. That's the way they work. Maybe the marshal can make Baker tell him who it was. Here comes the marshal now."

The town marshal listened to a dozen chattering voices, glanced at Slow Baker, who had lapsed into semi-consciousness, and approached Slade.

"Keeping up with your reputation, eh?" he said, with a grin. "Rolf Harty'll get a whoop outa this one. Did you ever have a run-in with those two hellions before?"

"Never saw them before, never heard of them," Slade replied. The marshal nodded.

"Just as I thought," he said. "Somebody put them up to it —hired them to do for you. They never go looking for trouble on their own account. That's what's kept them from stretching rope before now—somebody pulling wires for them. They could have gotten by with this one, the chances are, after yelling out 'El Halcón.' That is if they hadn't run up *against* El Halcón. Reckon *they* never heard much about *you*. Well, I'll have Slow packed to the calaboose and get the doctor to patch him up. Maybe we can learn something from him."

"Perhaps, but I doubt it," Slade answered.

Francia was tugging at his sleeve. "Please, dear, come and have your arm cared for," she pleaded. "You're bleeding terribly."

"Okay, if you insist," Slade deferred to her anxiety.

"I do insist," she said firmly. "I'll send for the doctor."

"No need to send for the doctor," Slade protested. "Stiffy will attend to it—just a scratch."

"You come along and stop arguing with me!" she exclaimed.

"Better do as the lady says," grinned the marshal. "She packs a whip."

In the kitchen, Slade removed his shirt to show the bullet slice in his upper arm. Francia cried out at sight of it, but Stiffy only chuckled.

"Betcha he's cut himself worse than that shaving," he declared as he procured salve and bandage, Francia hovering over them as he smeared, padded and bandaged the cut with his deft old hands.

"I'm going out and get you a drink," she said. "Stiffy, fix him some coffee."

"So, you've tamed her, eh?" chortled the cook. "Didn't think it was possible, although I *was* beginning to wonder a mite. After all, guess she's just a woman."

"I won't argue that," Slade smiled.

"Guess you won't," chuckled Stiffy. "Here's the coffee. You can put the whiskey in it. Mighty good for a feller who's lost some blood. That's what old-timers call a coffee royal."

Slade drank the spiced coffee, with Francia beside him. Then he donned his shirt and rolled a cigarette.

"Nice to be looked after," he told her. "You're a gal to ride the river with, or to—be with at any time."

Francia giggled and blushed, and hurried out to confer with Burk, the head bartender. Stiffy turned to Slade.

"Well, what do you think?" he asked.

"Stiffy," Slade replied soberly, "it's one devil of a thing to think of anybody, but—what do you think?"

"Mighty apt to be the same as you do," Stiffy replied. "Fact is, I'm not overly surprised. The hellion is poison. Both of 'em are, for that matter, and I don't know which is the worse. They've had folks fooled for quite a while, but not me, altogether. As you've guessed, of course, I did a bit of mavericking in my time and associated with that sort of cattle. I know 'em, maybe as well as you do. I ain't got your

69

brains, but I've had a heck of a lot of experience. You can't fool an old man who spent forty years of his life, or close to it, in the company of that kind. I can spot 'em a mile off. Just as," he added with a smile and a twinkle of his pale blue eyes, "just as I knew right away you don't belong to the owlhoot brand despite the El Halcón talk. In fact, I've got a mighty good notion of what you really are. Don't tell me—I'd rather not hear it. Just let me draw my own conclusions and let it go at that. Sometimes it's not best to know certain things for sure. No sense of a feller talking on responsibility he don't have to.

"And getting back to what we were talking about, do you happen to know anybody else who might have the sort of a grudge against you that would cause them to send hired killers looking for you?"

Slade shook his head. "Nobody I can think of who would fit into that category," he admitted.

"Then I think that just about tightens the twine," said Stiffy. "Now, anyhow, you know who to keep an eye on."

"Yes, now I have a fairly good notion who to keep an eye on, and who to look for.

"There's one jigger I sort of have a feud with, but he's the kind that looks after his own killings and doesn't hand the chore to somebody else unless it's a case of absolute necessity," he added retrospectively. "He wouldn't get any real pleasure from that method. And I'm sure he's down Mexico way right now; that's where he was headed for the last time I got a glimpse of him."

"Who's that?" Stiffy asked.

"Veck Sosna, the Panhandle outlaw and Comanchero leader," Slade said. Stiffy nodded.

As he spoke, Slade's glance shifted to the window, which had a southern exposure, and it seemed to Stiffy that his gaze traveled on and on, to the blue mounains of Sinaloa, far to the south.

"Nobody up here packs any authority down there," he observed irrelevantly. Slade turned from the window and smiled.

"The only authority down there that's worth a hang is what a man packs on his hip," he said. Stiffy nodded again.

Francia came in. "I'm hungry," she announced. "Come along, Walt, there's a table over by the corner of the dance floor where we can talk. Everybody's at the bar, jabbering about what happened."

As they crossed the room together, admiring glances were cast in their direction and heads drew together. Francia giggled.

"The gossips are having a regular round-up day," she whispered.

"Discussing the shooting, no doubt," Slade replied.

"Not likely, now," Francia differed. "They don't pay shootings much mind unless they happen to be mixed up in them. The taming of the hellcat is a much more engrossing subject."

"Really just a fluffy little kitten," Slade said as they sat down.

Francia laughed, but immediately she was serious.

"Walt," she said, "I have a confession to make. I've known for some time that you are El Halcón. I wheedled it out of Miguel. He pledged me to secrecy, but I think now I'm free to tell you. That's why I was so worried when the sheriff was talking to you; I was afraid he would—arrest you."

Slade's eyes danced with merriment. "I don't think you need bother your very pretty head on that score," he comforted her.

"Those terrible men who tried to kill you," she sighed.

"They made a mistake," he said shortly.

"But you are so alone."

Slade arrived at a sudden decision. From a cunningly concealed secret pocket he drew something and cupped it in his hands for her to see. It was a gleaming silver star set on a silver circle, the feared and honored badge of the Texas Rangers.

Francia gazed at the symbol of law and order, and for justice to all.

"I'm not so surprised as you might think," she said slowly. "You are just what I've always heard a Texas Ranger is like. We hear of them even in Arizona, where we have some Rangers of our own."

Slade nodded and replaced the badge. "So you see I'm not as alone as you think," he said. "I have all the power and prestige of the great State of Texas back of me, if I happen to need them."

"I think," Francia replied, "that you will never need them."

71

"I appreciate your confidence," he smiled. "I hope you'll always be right. Suppose we have something to eat?"

Just as they were finishing their dinner, the town marshal entered. He spotted them and approached the table. Francia told him to have a chair and beckoned a waiter.

"Well, we've got old Slow Baker all safe and comfy in the calaboose," the marshal announced as he accepted a drink. "The doctor gave him something or other with a needle to keep him quiet and he's sorta in a stupor. I haven't had a chance to talk with him, yet."

"Badly hurt?" Slade asked. The marshal shook his head.

"Nothing to pay much mind to, I reckon, or so Doc said. Low down through the shoulder, no bones busted. Painful, I guess, but not dangerous. I'll have a talk with him after a while."

"Let me know if you learn anything interesting," Slade requested.

The marshal promised to do so, downed his drink and departed.

"I think," Slade said, "that I'll ride in tomorrow with you and find out if the marshal learned anything. That is, if it's all right with you."

"Why ask me?" Francia retorted.

"Well, I'm working for you, am I not?"

"Theoretically, I suppose," she replied. "But *I'm* always taking orders from *you.*"

"Would you have it different?"

"No, darn it!" she answered with vigor. "I like it." A little later she asked, "Walt, why did those two men try so hard to kill you?"

"Their guns are, or were for hire," he replied noncommittally.

"You mean somebody hired them to kill you?"

"So I presume."

"Have you any idea who it is?"

"I'm not at the present prepared to name names," Slade parried. "But this much I will tell you. When the man is uncovered, which will give folks considerable of a surprise, I think the man who killed your brother and your range boss will also be uncovered."

Francia shuddered. "And those are the kind of people you go up against. They'll try again."

72

"Well, they didn't have much luck today."

"No, but they'll keep on trying."

"Once too often I expect."

"I don't doubt it," she conceded, "but just the same it isn't nice to have to think about it."

"Don't worry," he said. "Things will work out."

"Darn it! how can I keep from worrying?" she wailed but in low tones. "Oh, well, it looks like a slow night here. We'll go home early and forget our troubles."

"Sleep, that knits up the raveled sleeve of care," Slade slightly misquoted. Francia lowered her lashes, "Sleep?"

TWELVE

WHEN THEY REACHED THE SALOON the following afternoon, Stiffy had news for them.

"Well, your *amigo* Baker is out of jail," he announced to Slade.

"Somebody bail out the hellion?" the Ranger asked. Stiffy shook his head.

"Not exactly," he answered. "Last night the marshal went in to see how he was making out, and left the front door open. Two gents with handkerchiefs over their faces and guns in their hands walked in behind the marshal. They took his keys, unlocked the cell door and turned Baker loose. Marshal said the side-winder 'peared quite chipper. Reckon he'd been doing a little chore of 'possum playing when he pretended to be sorta hazy. The two fellers gagged the marshal and hog-tied him, and locked *him* in the cell. Baker wanted to kill him, but the two jiggers wouldn't go for that—scared of making a racket, maybe. They walked out, Baker with them.

"Took the marshal quite a while to get the gag out of his mouth and yell for help, and a while longer before somebody came to turn him loose. Had to cut off the lock with a hacksaw; fellers took the keys with them. Wasn't a sign of Baker or the two gents anywhere. Reckon they trailed their twine outa town."

"Logical to think so," Slade conceded dryly.

"What do you think of it?" asked Stiffy.

"I think somebody was afraid Baker might do some talking to save his own neck," El Halcón replied.

"My sentiments," said Stiffy.

Francia's eyes were worried, her face drawn. "Do you think that horrible Baker will try again to kill you?" she asked. Stiffy answered for Slade.

"Not that hyderphobia skunk. He had all of El Halcón he wants, a passel more. Old Slow will make himself scarce hereabouts, I reckon. He'll be thinking that maybe El Halcón will come looking for him. Bet he's sifting sand elsewhere right now."

Slade wasn't so sure, but he let it go at that. However, he was inclined to agree with Stiffy that Slow Baker would not come looking for him for personal reasons. A hired gunslinger usually takes defeat with the same philosophical shrug as any "businessman."

Anyhow, Baker's gun would be out of commission for a while.

However, that did not apply to the pair that sent Baker and Shotgun Blue on their chore of killing. They were enjoying excellent health, so far as Slade knew. Yes, he had a very good notion who they were, but the trouble was he had not one iota of proof against them. Certainly nothing that would stand up in court. He had hoped that Baker might be induced to talk in order to save himself, but now that was out. Well, maybe he'd get a break.

But how in blazes did the stolen cows cross the Tinaja Desert? He didn't have the answer to that one, either; but he was determined to learn it.

"Well, I guess I'd better be heading back to the spread," he said to Francia. "Try and keep out of trouble."

"Me keep out of trouble!" she exploded. "Suppose you try it for a change. Perhaps I shouldn't allow you to ride alone."

"You've been doing it every night for quite a while," he reminded her.

"Yes, but nobody's out to kill me, so far as I know. Anyhow, please be careful."

"I will," he promised. He glanced at her Levi's.

"You haven't changed yet," he observed.

"And I'm not going to," she retorted. "Oh, I read disapproval in your eyes. If I can't get along with overalls and a shirt, I'll—I'll—"

"Get along without them?"

For some reason best known to herself, the facetious remark caused her to blush hotly.

"You're impossible!" she exclaimed. "But please be careful."

Slade rode north out of town, but he didn't hold to that direction. As soon as he was well clear of the settlement he turned west, continued for a while, and then turned due south and slightly west after crossing the railroad. Soon the arid expanse of the Tinaja Desert, glowing in the late afternoon sunlight, was before him. At the edge of the sands he reined in, rolled a cigarette and sat gazing across the inhospitable terrain.

"Getting a mite cooler already," he observed to Shadow. "When the sun goes down it won't be bad out there. I figure it's a good idea to do the first half during the night, for I don't think there's much chance of running onto anything interesting until we are at least half way across. And even then it's likely to be considerable of a chore. If there's water anywhere out there it must be well hidden, or the fact would be of general knowledge. But Captain Arrington and his Rangers of the Panhandle found water on the Tucumcari desert when everybody insisted that there was none. He found the Lost Lakes, although they were way over in New Mexico instead of in Gaines County, Texas, as he thought.

"How did he do it? He found near a spring the bleached shoulder blade of a giant buffalo. On the smooth surface of that white blackboard of the High Plains were daubed figures and diagrams he was able to interpret. It was a signboard used by the Indians to direct those who were to follow to the water. Arrington followed the route indicated by the Indians and found water.

"Which brings to mind something else Indian. Old-timers insisted that the Indians used to drive stock clear across *this* desert to the Rio Grande and Mexico, and they couldn't have done it without water. So in my opinion there *is* water out there somewhere, and it's up to us to find it. If we do, we'll have a good chance to drop a loop on the hellions we're after. See?"

75

Shadow snorted resigned agreement and at a word from his master, moved out onto the hot sands.

As Slade predicted, the going wasn't too bad in the late afternoon. He let Shadow take his time, and as the sun sank lower, the heat appreciably decreased.

Fortunately, the weather was fine, with not a breath of air stirring. Had a hard wind been moving the sands and the alkali dust, it would have been a different matter. And Slade did not underestimate the danger of the desert in time of storm, especially if there was no rain to cool the air and lay the dust.

The stupendous sunset of the desert flamed its splendor over the western crags. Gently the twilight descended, faded to dusk. The dusk deepened to night. The silver roses of the sky blossomed in glowing beauty and the soft hush of the wastelands enfolded the lone rider, the silence broken only by —faint with distance—the lonely, hauntingly-beautiful plaint of a hunting wolf.

Slade rode slowly, for the night was very dark. Soon, however, a nearly full moon rose in the east, flooding the desert with ghostly light in which objects stood out in stark relief. Sand dunes reared their monstrous bulk, with now and then spires of rock that had defied the general erosion which lowered the desert floor.

The desert was not totally devoid of vegetation. There were cholla cacti and thorny shrubs, with occasional scatterings of dusty looking mesquite; the tremendous root system of which permitted it to survive on moisture stored up during the rains. And there were sparse growths of sage.

"Horse," he remarked, "there is water under the sand, and, I would say, at no great depth, the way such things are measured. But water a few hundred or a few thousand feet down won't do us much good."

Slade knew that all this section of Texas covered a vast underground water system that some day, properly taken advantage of, would cause such wastelands to blossom like the proverbial rose. History would prove his prediction. Subterranean water that sometimes manifested itself in peculiar ways.

By one o'clock in the morning he estimated that he was not far from half way across the wasteland and looked about for a place to camp, for he wished to cover the second leg of his journey in daylight.

76

A mesquite clump provided fuel for a fire and he made a dry camp. He had taken the precaution of filling his canteen with cold coffee, which soon was bubbling in a little flat bucket. A second canteen filled with water provided drink for Shadow, who meditatively munched shriveled mesquite pods which he apparently thought better than nothing. A double handful of oats from one of the pouches put him in a somewhat better temper.

Slade fixed bacon and eggs in a small skillet. A hunch of bread completed his simple meal, washed down with the steaming coffee. Then he smoked a cigarette and, after cleaning and storing the utensils, curled up beside the dying fire and soon was fast asleep, to be awakened by the rose and saffron beauty of the dawn.

A few bites of bread and some of the coffee he had saved passed as breakfast. Feeling fit for anything, he saddled up and rode on through the increasing heat, slowly, for he was carefully studying his surroundings.

The desert was not altogether flat. There were swales and low ridges, where the intensity of the heat varied. Climbing one of the slopes to its crest, he halted the black horse for a moment. He was gazing down into a shallow bowl almost circular in shape and perhaps a mile in diameter. He didn't particularly like the looks of the ominous appearing depression but it cut across the route he wished to follow, so he sent Shadow down the opposite slope and reached the bottom. He shook his head disapprovingly.

"Although a great deal smaller, it sorta reminds one of the bottom of Death Valley in California, doesn't it, horse?" he remarked.

Shadow snorted equine profanity and slogged on.

Rising from the floor of the bowl near its center were three large sand dunes. They were not overly high but very broad at the base, with gently sloping sandy sides that looked more stable than the fluffy stuff which surfaced the floor of the bowl.

In the depths, the heat was intense and Slade was glad when they surmounted the opposite sag and reached the higher elevation of the main desert floor.

"Wouldn't want to have to stay in that hole too long," he told Shadow; "it's deadly."

77

He rode on and on, scanning his surroundings with the greatest care.

They were decidedly unsatisfactory. On all sides stretched the profitless waste of sand and alkali, with not a sight of anything that remotely resembled water or the possibility of its presence.

"But blast it! I know the critters came this way," he growled aloud. "And with anything like luck I'm going to prove that, anyhow, before we reach the river. But as to how they did it, I still don't know. And already we've covered just about as much distance as they could possibly travel in one night of fast going. Oh, well, horse, we're not used to packing a licking, and we're not going to pack one now; we'll keep on trying till we hit paydirt."

It was getting along toward midday when, after climbing a long rise and reaching the crest, he saw in the distance the flash and shimmer of the Rio Grande. He pulled up and sat gazing toward the river, experiencing an irritating sense of frustration. Nothing could have been more meticulous than his examination of the terrain over which he had passed; and no examination could have been more barren of results.

On the surface of the slope up which Shadow had just toiled, the sand and alkali had given way to hard packed clay. Now the soil was still clay, the belt extending for a quarter of a mile or so before being supplanted by grassland. But here the clay was much softer. Slade eyed it with satisfaction.

After giving Shadow a time for a breather in the now much cooler air, he headed for the river. And again he rode in long, sharp-angled zig-zags, quartering the ground with care. Suddenly he uttered an exclamation and halted Shadow, staring at the ground at his feet.

"Horse, I was right," he said. "Here they are, here they passed. This clay holds prints indefinitely. Cows and horses, a lot of cows. Some of the marks are comparatively new, some of them quite old. Get going, feller."

Straight to the grassland the tracks led. On the pasture they were invisible, but their direction was certain. And when he pulled up on the lip of the river bank, they were clearly discernible on the softer and sparsely grown soil which edged the stream.

He gazed in exasperation at the impassive river, which

78

seemed to mock him with its ripple and flow. As if it could divulge the secret if it would. Which it didn't.

Slade and Shadow drank their fill of the waters of *Resaca de la Palma*, the River of the Palms, although there were certainly no palms in evidence here. He removed the rig and allowed the horse to roll and graze. Then he stretched out on the grass and enjoyed several leisurely cigarettes. After which he saddled up, tightened his belt over his own empty stomach and rode north. He had had enough of the desert for the time being and intended to keep to the grasslands on the return trip. It would mean a longer ride but a much more comfortable and safe one. Best not take chances on the infernal wastelands with a horse that was already tired. He had been fortunate where the weather was concerned, but that could change swiftly and he had no desire to be caught in a storm. Here the air was cool and pleasant, the going easy.

Nevertheless, it was long past midnight when, thoroughly worn out and Shadow's gait reduced to a shamble, he reached the Rocking T ranchhouse.

Francia came flying out on the porch to greet him. "Where in heaven's name have you been?" she demanded. "I've been worried sick. Why didn't you tell me you were going off on some hare-brained expedition?"

"I didn't want you to worry," he explained.

Francia stamped one small foot vigorously. "Didn't want me to worry!" she stormed. "If that isn't just like a man. Could I have worried more than I did when you seemingly vanished into thin air? Come in, I have hot coffee and something to eat for you."

"After I look after my horse," he agreed.

Making sure that Shadow was properly cared for and all his wants provided against, he walked wearily to the house. Francia had drawn a small and low table beside his favorite chair and was placing coffee and food on it.

"So you can relax comfortably while you're eating," she said.

"You don't know what you're doing to me," he protested. "Spoiling me completely."

"Huh! look what you've done to me!" she retorted. "Taken away my short pants and my open-front shirt, and—my whip."

"You've discarded that, too?"

79

"Of course. You didn't approve of it. The lookout keeps order now. He has an easy chore. He just walks up to a bunch that appears to be getting out of hand and says, 'Want to have El Halcón come looking for you? What he packs is a lot worse than a whip.' He gets order."

Tired as he was, Slade had to laugh. Quickly, however, he was sober.

"I think," he said, "that you would do well to sell the saloon and devote all your energies to running the ranch as it should be run."

"And you'd really prefer me to do so?"

"I would."

"Very well," she sighed. "I'll do it. I can't refuse you anything."

"So I've found out," he replied, his eyes crinkling at the corners.

THIRTEEN

SLADE RODE THE RANGE the following day and was pleased with the amount of work accomplished and the progress made during his absence.

"Yep, we're rolling along," said Sime Collins. "A couple more days and we'll have the last brand run on the chore. By the way, Sid Gholen says he lost some cows the other night. Swears he's going to patrol his holding at night from now on. Hope he does, the hellions have to drive the cows across his land to reach the slopes."

"Yes, they have to cross his land," Slade agreed soberly.

He was due to hear more of the doings of Mr. Gholen. Francia came in from a morning ride to town in a puzzled frame of mind.

"I was at the bank today, to pay the interest on the mortgage," she told Slade. "Mr. Warburton, the president, said they didn't own the mortgage any more. They sold it."

"Who to?" Slade asked.

"To Sid Gholen. He said that Sid said he considered it a

good investment and that it would be to my advantage, seeing as I wouldn't have any difficulty getting extensions if I happened to need them. Mr. Warburton admitted that a bank that is land poor as his is can go just so far. I happen to know they have got a lot of money tied up in land mortgages, and I've a notion some of them are a bit shaky. He said they would have notified me of the sale, through courtesy, although they wouldn't have to; such a mortgage is negotiable and can be bought or sold without notifying the mortgagor."

"That's right," Slade nodded. "And Gholen bought it. Hmmm!"

Francia looked pensive. "Sid once asked me to marry him," she remarked with apparent irrelevance.

"Yes? And what was your answer?"

"I told him no, very shortly, for at that time I was still Francia the hellcat, and didn't have to mince words. Some folks think he would be a good catch, but I never could see him in that light. He had a way of looking at me that caused my skin to creep. It wasn't exactly a nice way for a man to look at a woman."

"Meaning?"

"Meaning it was a sort of appraising look, the kind of a look you bestow on a head of stock you are contemplating owning. A woman doesn't mind a man looking at her with desire in his eyes, even though the desire may be a bit off-color. That she'll excuse, admitting it might be her own fault —she asked for it—but the look in Sid Gholen's eyes always made me bristle. Why? I don't know. Call it feminine intuition, if you will."

"Feminine intuition is the counterpart of a man's hunch." Slade observed. "And very often it is based on subconscious reasoning that is hard to explain but nevertheless exists. You made a wise decision."

Francia dimpled at him. "You're telling me? And if a decision sometimes may not be so wise, it can be very satisfying, for a while."

"For a while?"

"Yes, as I told you once before, for a while. But just the same, I'll never regret."

"Perhaps you may never need to."

The dimple vanished and her face became somber. "Any-

81

how, one can hope. Oh, well, today is today. I'll make us some coffee."

While the coffee was being brewed, Slade pondered Sid Gholen's unexpected move. The explanation was simple. Gholen expected to eventually acquire the Rocking T. Added to his own land, it would be just about the best and most potentially prosperous holding in the section. The catch, of course, was equally simple—a spread without cows can't hope to remain solvent, and the Rocking T stock had already been dangerously depleted. A few more successful raids and Francia would be unable to meet the note when it fell due with foreclosure the next move; Gholen getting title for much less than the actual worth of the ranch. It was highly unlikely that anybody would bid against him and raise the ante, for as the banker said, the section was land poor—too much land for the needs of the majority of the owners; they wouldn't be interested in acquiring more, especially if it could not be linked with their present holdings. Well, he'd see about that.

As they drank the coffee together, Francia suddenly said, "Walt, are you going to again take that awful ride across the desert?"

"Guess I'll have to," he replied. "I've got to find out how they get the cows across."

She was silent for several moments, then, "Dear, will you do me a really big favor?"

"Of course, if I can," he answered. "What is it?"

"Let me go with you. I can ride and I can shoot. I won't be any trouble, and I might be able to help—never can tell. Please!"

Slade hesitated before answering. After all, however, there was really very little danger attached to the venture. The only real hazard was the possibility of a sudden storm. Which was really unlikely. Usually there was a build-up that preceded and warned of inclement weather.

"What about your business in town?" he demurred.

"Burk, the head bartender, has already taken over most of my responsibilities," she replied. "I think he would like to buy the place, if we can get together on terms."

Slade chuckled inwardly. He could picture Sid Gholen's pawing sod if he learned he had the burly, shrewd and salty Burk to deal with.

"All right," he said. "I'll take a chance on you. But I aim

82

to do more than half of the desert by daylight this time. You're liable to have a warm time of it before we get across."

"I wouldn't be surprised," Francia giggled.

"Now who's being impossible?" he demanded. Francia shrugged.

"Well, a girl can dream, can't she?"

Slade thought it best not to try to frame an answer. Francia asked, "When do you plan to go?"

"I haven't definitely decided," he replied. "I want to think things over a bit and recall everything I saw that was in the least out of the ordinary."

"From what you told me, I'd say that awful sunken bowl where the heat was so terrible was out of the ordinary," Francia observed.

Slade gazed at her, his black brows drawing together until the concentration furrow was deep between them.

"Honey," he said, "all of a sudden you have given me something definite to think on."

"Didn't I say I might be a help?" she exclaimed triumphantly.

"Beginning to look like you are even before we start," he admitted.

Francia jumped to her feet. "Here come the boys for supper," she exclaimed. "You must be ready to eat, too; all you've had is coffee. No, I'm not going in to the place tonight. It'll be slow and Burk will take care of everything. Maybe I can persuade you to play and sing for me."

After supper, Slade went to the barn to make sure that Shadow was okay, and to commune with the big black.

"Horse," he said, "the little girl may have given us a straight tip. Remember, we once contacted something that could be paralleled to that infernal hot hole we crossed in a hurry without paying much attention to details. That sunken bowl undoubtedly means subsidence sometimes in past ages. And subsidence could conceivably exert pressure on subterranean water. Horse, that could be it. And Pete knows we didn't sight anything else that looked in the least promising. No rock formations with caves that might lead to water. No indications that water might be somewhere just below the surface. Well, we'll play the hunch and see if it works out."

Slade was due to take a trip onto the desert sooner than he anticipated, and a highly unpleasant one.

There were still some critters holed up in the coulees and brakes to the south, especially young stuff, and Sime Collins had been complaining querulously over the calf tally.

"I tell you they're robbing us blind, the blankety-blank-blanks!" he told Slade. "We ain't showing up anything like what we should. Something's got to be done about it." To which Slade wholeheartedly agreed.

"We'll take a ride down to the southwest and see what's left there," he said. "We should be able to get something of a check and send the boys to where they can do the best chore of combing out."

So in the early afternoon they set out. Francia wished to accompany them and Slade saw no reason why she should not. She appeared to have completely lost interest in the saloon. Besides, the arrangements for Burk to take over were almost completed.

It was a beautiful day when dying summer was garbed in her deepest blues flecked with scarlet and gold. To the southwest, close to the horizon, was a bank of cloud, but otherwise the sky was a clear sun-washed arch of cerulean.

They rode slowly, making a spot check of all the cattle they saw. Now and then they would meet one of the hands driving a bunch, mostly calves and yearlings, to the north. After a while, however, they reached the southernmost point of present operations.

After quite a few miles of riding they neared a long straggle of grove that stretched east and west across the prairie, and diagonaled toward its western fringe.

Suddenly Slade uttered an exclamation. "Now what's going on down the other side of those trees?" he remarked.

"I don't see nothing," replied Collins. "You spotted something?"

"Yes," Slade said, "smoke."

"Smoke? I don't see any," said the old waddie, puckering his eyes against the sun glare.

It was indeed but a tiny wisp of lighter blue against the blue of the sky, but the eyes of El Halcón had not deceived him. A moment later Collins also was able to make it out. Slade quickened Shadow's pace a little.

"Something going on down there," he observed. "We'll soon find out what—I've got a notion."

They rounded the scattering of trunks where the grove petered out and saw the origin of the smoke. A small fire of dry wood had been kindled, and beside the fire squatted two men. Stretched on the ground was something that Slade instantly recognized as a year-old calf. It was held motionless by the ropes stretched from two standing horses.

"Thought so," the Ranger said. Collins, forgetting Francia's presence, swore explosively.

Evidently the two men had seen them round the edge of the grove, for they stood up. One removed his hat and waved it in a circle, the universally recognized signal of the range, "Keep going and mind your own business!"

"Waving us around, eh?" Slade said. "We'll see about that."

"Slick-iron artists sure as blazes!" whooped Collins. "They're running a burn on one of our critters. Told you they were robbin' us blind. Let's go!"

From where the two men stood came a puff of whitish smoke. A bullet whined past overhead. Then another.

"So you want to play rough, eh?" Slade said. "Come on, Sime. Francia, stay back."

He sent Shadow forward swiftly, sliding his Winchester from the saddle boot as he did so. Still another slug split the air above their heads. Collins swore and flung up his rifle.

"Hold it!" Slade warned. "Get a little closer." Collins ducked instinctively as a bullet whistled past, close.

Slade clamped the butt of the Winchester against his shoulder, his voice rang out, "Steady, Shadow, steady!"

Instantly the big black leveled off in a smooth running walk. Slade glanced along the sights and squeezed the trigger.

One of the men ducked even as Collins had. Slade lowered the rifle muzzle the merest trifle.

"Closer to them than I thought," he muttered and squeezed the trigger. This time he believed he saw one of the men lurch, but wasn't sure. Collins was blazing away wildly and swearing at the top of his voice.

For the third time, Slade squeezed the trigger; and now he had the range.

One of the slick-ironers pitched forward across the fire and lay there smoking. The other scooped up something from the ground, raced to one of the standing houses, cut the rope that tethered it to the prostrate calf, flung himself into the hull and sent his mount speeding southward toward the now not so distant desert.

"Take care of that one on the ground," Slade shouted to Collins. "Francia, stay with Sime!"

He settled himself in the saddle. Again his voice rang out, "Trail, Shadow, trail!"

Instantly the great horse extended himself, blowing, snorting, slugging his head above the bit, and the race was on.

FOURTEEN

MILE AFTER MILE flowed back under the drumming hoofs. But the slick-ironer was well mounted and though Shadow steadily closed the gap, he closed it slowly. The quarry's near six hundred yard lead shrank to five-fifty, to five hundred. Rifle range for El Halcón.

Under other circumstances, Slade would have been tempted to risk a long shot or two, although that would mean losing some of the distance gained. But he earnestly desired to just wing the fellow, take him alive and try to induce him to talk. So he held his fire and urged Shadow to greater speed.

Now the desert, for which the outlaw was evidently heading, was only a couple of miles away, and Slade saw something that threatened to bring his plan to naught. The cloud bank which had been but a dark line on the horizon had climbed to nearly midway to the zenith, and with it came a steadily freshening wind. It felt unpleasantly like a storm wind, Slade thought. And already the face of the desert was growing misty. Which meant the sands were moving under the beat of the wind, the dust rising. If the wind grew much stronger, soon it would be flying in blinding clouds.

Once he glanced over his shoulder to see, far behind, the rising and falling dots that were his two companions, hopelessly outdistanced.

Now Shadow was closing the gap; his greater endurance

was paying off. Not more than three hundred yards separated the racing horses. Slade fingered the stock of the rifle, decided to wait a little longer. Maybe the fugitive wouldn't dare the desert with every indication of a storm approaching.

But he did. He reached the beginning of the sands and kept going. It dawned on the Ranger that very likely he knew of some refuge out there on the alkali wastes and was making for it; where perhaps he had companions who would come to his rescue. Again he fingered the rifle as Shadow reached the sands; but he realized he had waited too long. The slick-ironer was now but a blurred shape amid the dust and in the uncertain light. To attempt to drill an arm or leg would be based on the merest guesswork.

"Okay," he growled, "If you can take it, I can." Eventually he would get near enough to risk a shot, that is, if the whole blasted desert didn't blow up in his face; there were uncomfortable indications that it would do just that.

Slade knew he was taking a chance in following the quarry onto the desert, but he grimly kept on, feeling that he and the fellow had to play the hand out.

"We've done it before, and we can do it again—maybe," he told Shadow, who snorted his disgust but never faltered. Slade flopped down the brim of his hat all around to keep the sand from collecting on it, pulled up his neckerchief and muffled it over his nose and mouth; breathing was already becoming difficult. But he could still see the misty form of the fugitive; Shadow was still closing the distance.

Now, however, the wind had risen to almost gale force and a full-fledged storm was roaring across the Tinaja. The air was hot, the flying grains of sand stung the skin like flecks of fire. Yellow shadows swooped and curdled. The sun was a queer magenta color, like to a blood-red orange or the full moon seen low down on the horizon through haze. Slade felt his mouth growing leathery and he knew his lips were beginning to crack, his tongue to swell slightly. Danger signals the desert-wise knew should not be disregarded.

They were several miles out on the wind-torn waste and exposed to the full fury of the storm. But still the horse in front staggered on, with Shadow shambling after him and slowly but surely closing the distance. Slade reached for his rifle; he'd take a chance on a shot. To keep on going under such conditions was sheer lunacy. And at that moment the outlaw gave it up. He whirled his mount to face his pursuer. The gun he held spouted flame as Slade swayed far sideways in the saddle, and felt the bullet fan his face. Then his own guns let go with a rattling crash.

There was little chance to take aim; it was almost blind shooting, shadow at shadow through the swirling yellow murk. Slade counted his shots; his guns were dangerously near to being empty. The outlaw had drawn a second gun and was blazing away with that.

Suddenly he gave a wailing cry that ended in a gurgling whimper. He reeled, lurched, slumped forward, both hands flinging up, then slid slowly sideways from the saddle to lie on his back, the sand sifting down a gritty shroud that would soon hide him from view.

Slade sent Shadow forward a few more paces, pulled him to a halt and swung to the ground on legs that seemed strangely wooden. He lurched to where the outlaw lay, his hard-lined face contorted in the agony of death. His features were strange to Slade.

"Never saw him before, I'm sure," he muttered to Shadow. He risked emptying the fellow's pockets but found nothing of interest. Then he straightened up, and with effort swung into the saddle. He turned Shadow's nose, whistled the outlaw's horse, which obediently lurched after him.

Slade was not feeling any too good, but he was not particularly apprehensive. He'd had plenty of desert experience and knew how to husband his strength and that of his mount. Slow and easy, but never halt. The lethargy engendered by heat and difficult breathing could be as deadly as that caused by extreme cold. Pause but briefly and one might well succumb to it. So he hunched forward in the saddle, breathed easily and encouraged the horse with voice and hand.

Suddenly he raised his head in an attitude of listening. From somewhere ahead had come three evenly spaced shots —the wasteland's call for help, or to guide the lost one to safety. With an exasperated exclamation he drew one of his guns and answered the signal. Evidently Sime Collins had followed him onto the desert; he'd hoped the experienced old-timer would have better sense.

Again came three shots, closer. He fired again, spacing the shots a little more, peered and listened.

A form loomed directly ahead, vague, distorted, drew

nearer, and Slade saw it was Francia, coughing and gasping.

"You little idiot!" he stormed at her. "Why the devil did you come out here?"

"You—you were out here," she replied simply, between spells of coughing.

"But, blast it, I'm used to it!" he said. He reached out, jerked her neckerchief off her throat and muffled it over her nose and mouth.

"Breathe slowly," he told her. "Slow and deep. Keep your mouth shut, tight, and breathe through your nose. Lean forward and relax. Don't try to guide your horse—he'll stay with Shadow. Easy, now, we'll make it, if the horses hold out. Shadow is a good desert horse and will do all right. I only hope the others will be okay. Don't talk, now, save all your energy. Breathe deep. And breathe slow."

She did as she was told. Slade kept Shadow close to her staggering bay, so that he could pluck her from the saddle if the laboring animal should fall. The outlaw's horse was still following and, carrying no burden, was likely to make it, Slade thought. But he was frankly dubious as to Francia's mount; it appeared to be in real distress, and he dreaded to subject Shadow to the extra burden of even her slight weight.

They shambled on, and gradually Slade began to be haunted by that senseless but all too real fear that envelops the wanderer in a desert storm—the fear that his sense of direction is at fault, and he is drifting farther and farther into the deadly waste instead of progressing toward safety. He strove to shake it off, but it persisted, developing the almost unbearable urge to charge forward at top speed, the act of a lunatic that could end only in death.

But with the iron hand of will he held the terrible spectre off, talking to his horse, his voice but a hoarse croak, watching the girl at his side, who slumped forward in the saddle, breathing slowly and deeply as he told her, but in hoarse gasps.

He saw her try to straighten, sway sideways. But before she fell, his arm was around her, jerking her feet free from the stirrups, hugging her close to him, her face against his shirt front.

"Don't move," he warned. "Stay perfectly relaxed. We'll make it."

"I—I shouldn't have come," she breathed. "but I wanted —to—help—"

89

"Don't talk," he interrupted. "Save your strength. You meant for the best. Don't talk."

She relaxed into near unconsciousness. Slade held her close and rode on through the inferno of heat and dust. The bay, relieved of her weight, appeared to have picked up a bit. But her added weight was telling on Shadow. Now and then he stumbled, his head hanging, the breath whistling through his flaring nostrils; Slade was beginning to get badly worried. Again that rush of fear that he was going the wrong way, although his plainsman's instinct told him he was still headed north. Just the same, a numb feeling of despair was gripping his heart with clammy fingers. Shadow couldn't take much more, and should he fall, it was the end.

Abruptly the sand cloud thinned. Another moment and Slade breathed great draughts of life-giving air that was free from dust. Behind him the storm roared angrily and the cloud of flying sand seemed to strain after them, futilely.

The two horses had followed to safety, Slade was glad to see. But he realized that he had an utterly exhausted girl in his arms. Her eyes were closed and there was hardly any color on her lips that normally were so vividly red.

He glanced anxiously about, saw a waterhole a few hundred yards farther to the north and made for it. Dismounting, he placed Francia on the grass at its edge, fetched water in his hat and bathed her wrists and temples. She opened her eyes and gazed up at him. He slipped an arm under her shoulders.

"Are we dead?" she asked dreamily. "If so, I'm in Heaven."

"Guess you've still got a long ways to go," he chuckled. "But for a while I wasn't so sure; was too close to taking the Big Jump to be pleasant. Think you can sit up?"

"Sure, I'm all right now," she said, suiting the action to the word, Slade supporting her, and drank from the hat.

"Now take it easy while I look after the cayuses," he said.

The horses had plunged their noses into the water to drink and drink. After quenching their thirst, the bay and the outlaw's mount immediately lay down. Shadow, water dripping from his lower lip, snorted disdain at such weakness and began to graze. Slade flipped out the bit and left him to his own devices, which apparently consisted of a determination to fill his stomach as quickly as possible.

A shout sounded in the distance. Slade turned and saw

Sime Collins riding toward them from the west. The old waddie let out a joyous whoop.

"Blazes! I'm glad to see you!" he bellowed. "I was getting bad scared for you. I tried to keep her from following you, Slade, but there was no stopping her. I knew you'd take care of her and stayed out myself. Figured I'd just be making more trouble for you if I went along."

"You used your head," Slade complimented him. "No place for anybody not accustomed to desert storms."

"Did the hellion get away?" Collins asked, glancing at the outlaw's horse.

"Out there under the sand," Slade replied soberly. "Did you learn anything from the other one?"

"Naw," Sime answered disgustedly. "Never saw the sidewinder before. Mean-looking cuss. They hadn't marked the cow yet and I couldn't find the branding iron. Reckon the other one took it with him. I thought I saw him pick up something as he high-tailed for his horse."

"Evidently threw it away in the desert," Slade decided. "Didn't have it on him. A pity, it might have given us some valuable evidence."

"Would have told us who's doing the stealing, I reckon," Collins growled. "The other feller's horse had a Mexican burn like that one."

"Which means nothing," Slade said. "Well, anyhow we bagged a couple, which means something. How you feeling now, Francia?"

"I'm okay, only awful thirsty," the girl replied.

"Soon take care of that," Slade said cheerfully and fetched more water, as much as he thought she should have, in his hat. After which he had a couple of swigs himself.

"Guess we might as well head for home as soon as your horse puts away a surrounding," he said, gesturing to the bay which, along with the dead slick-ironer's mount, was on its feet and grazing. "Been quite an afternoon, but all's well that ends well, as the saying goes."

"See, now, why I hesitated to agreeing to let you go with me across the desert," he added in low tones as Collins moved away to care for his cayuse.

"Yes, but now I'm more determined than ever to go, if you'll let me," she replied. "I'd go crazy with you out there alone."

"Okay," he chuckled. "So we'll go crazy together."

"Won't be the first time," Francia giggled. "Could I have some more water?"

FIFTEEN

IT WAS DARK when they reached the ranchhouse, but with the elasticity of youth they had both thrown off the effects of their harrowing experience and aside from being ravenous, were fit for anything.

The hands listened with interest and muttered profanity to old Sime's graphic account of the day's happenings and professed fervent hope that they'd get a chance at the blankety-blank-blank who was back of the hell raising.

"But who in blazes is it?" somebody demanded. Another shrugged.

"Quite a few new folks over to the west," he observed pointedly.

"Uh-huh, but there's nothing to tie them up with it no more than anybody else, so far as we've been able to learn," Sime Collins pointed out. "They 'pear to be okay, those of 'em I've run into, but of course, sometimes there's a rotten apple in a barrel."

The others nodded agreement. Slade did not comment.

However, he was pondering the situation seriously. Such operations could be disastrous for the owner. Nothing spectacular, just the slick-ironing of a calf or a yearling now then. Just the running off of a score or so of beef critters. Enough of it, though, and the owner was out of business. The simplest of arithmetic applied to cattle raising. Outlay is so much and is met by the cows sold. More cow returns than outlay and you're okay. Not enough cows for sale to meet the expenses and very quickly you are finished. A big owner with a reserve of cash could stand it for a while, although not indefinitely. The small owner would go under more quickly. He definitely couldn't take it.

The Rocking T was typical; the calf crop was not what it should be, and there was likely to be a scarcity of shipping beef when the Fall round-up was over. And Francia was worried about the five thousand dollars she felt she owed Sid Gholen. Well, she wouldn't have to worry about that if things worked out the way he hoped they would. He chuckled at the thought of Gholen holding the mortgage on the spread. Now she wouldn't have to pay that, either. That is, again, if things worked out the way he hoped they would and expected they would.

There was no doubt in Slade's mind but that Sid Gholen was the mastermind back of the extensive cattle stealing which had plagued the section. Also that Gholen was the head of the bunch he, Slade, had been sent to clean out.

Which was fine, except that he had not a scintilla of proof against Gholen. Certainly nothing that would stand up in court. Gholen had slipped badly and had given Slade his first real lead when he brought in the two professional gunmen, Slow Baker and Shotgun Blue, to do away with El Halcón whom he undoubtedly considered a menace to his activities. Quite likely he believed that El Halcón, a fellow outlaw, aimed to take over the lucrative operation.

Yes, Gholen had made his second and perhaps fatal slip when he hired Baker and Shotgun Blue to do a chore of murder. His first slip had been the fight he picked with El Halcón, believing he could give him a good thrashing and then egg him into turning the fist fight into a corpse and cartridge session, in which he, Gholen, would shoot in self defense, aided and abetted by his sinister range boss, Alf Crane. And who would bother much about the demise of another owlhoot shot down by a reputable citizen of the community.

Gholen had scored when he managed to slide Baker out of jail before he had a chance to talk and save himself. Baker was either carefully holed up somewhere or dead, quite likely the latter.

The key to the solution, Slade was sure, lay somewhere in the Tinaja Desert. If he could only discover where the stolen cattle were laid over to drink and rest, there was every chance to set a trap for the outlaws and dispose of them. First, however, he had to locate the water on a desert where there was supposed to be none. Which might take considerable "locating," although he hopefully believed he had a clue to its whereabouts. Well, he'd soon find out.

He experienced a slight feeling of disquietude as he remembered that he had allowed Francia to talk him into taking her with him on the trip of discovery. However, it was only momentary; he could see no real reason why she should be endangered by the trip. About the only thing to bother his head about, so far as he could see, was the possibility of an unexpected storm; but he believed he was weatherwise enough to guard against that.

Painstakingly he reviewed, in his mind, the route he had followed across the desert. His retentive memory brought into sharp focus every ridge and swale and rock formation, and he searched them in minute detail for any possible significance. And very clear indeed was that ghastly bowl where the sun beat down with furnace heat and the alkali dust rose in stifling clouds under the beat of his horse's hoofs. With the three great dunes, not so high but very broad of base that stood in the midst of the desolation, austere, aloof, inscrutable. Like to Gizeh's pyramids amid the sands of Egypt, guarding an age-old secret and exuding a sinister threat for anyone who would dare to wrest it from them.

And that was just what El Halcón was determined to attempt. Francia's chance remark had set his mind working on that angle of the problem which confronted him, and the more he pondered it the more firmly he believed that she had unwittingly provided him with the solution of the mystery. Well, he'd see. If that wasn't it, he hadn't the slightest notion what was.

The cowboys ended their discussion and trooped off to bed. Slade and Francia were left alone in the living room.

"Suppose you come back to me for a little while," she suggested. "You've been miles away all evening. I'm almost tempted to believe it's some 'she' you've been thinking about."

"If it wasn't, it is now," he replied, smiling at her. "Really, though, I was thinking of our proposed trip across the desert. Still hanker to go along?"

"I certainly do," she declared, with emphasis. "You promised."

"I'll keep my promise," he said. "But if your classic nose gets sunburned and peels, don't blame me."

Francia used that member to produce a disdainful sniff. "Think your Texas sun is hot, do you? Just take a sashay

94

down around Yuma, Arizona, and see what you think," she challenged.

"I've been there, and it is hot," Slade conceded. "I heard that a citizen of Yuma died and went to Hades. Next day he sent back for his blankets."

"It isn't that bad, I guess, but it has been known to reach 120 in the shade, and no shade," Francia answered. "I don't believe your Tinaja Desert much can beat that."

"The Tinaja isn't too bad," Slade admitted. "I've seen worse. The Monahan Desert up to the north of here, for instance. That's a salt desert and is really bad. So I guess we'll make out."

For some moments, Francia regarded him in silence. Then, "Walt, are you still not of a mind to tell me whom you suspect as being the cause of our trouble here?"

"Francia," he replied, "because I'm firmly convinced in my own mind I'm right, I'll tell you. It's Sid Gholen."

Francia's reaction was calmer than he had expected.

"Call it a woman's intuition again, if you wish," she said, "but I'm not overly surprised. For no good reason I can put my finger on, I've never liked and never trusted him. As I told you, he *looks* at me. He smiles a lot, but his smile always strikes me as being more of a grimace than a smile. And Alf Crane, his range boss who is always with him, gives me the creeps. His eyes are like a snake's; I don't think I've ever seen him blink his lids."

"There is no such thing as a criminal physiognomy, contrary to popular belief, but there are certain characteristics that will bear watching," he said. "For instance, if you don't like a person's mouth—" Francia puckered hers suggestively— "don't have anything to do with him, or her. Do and you'll be sorry."

"I can understand that and I agree," she replied. "Now take your mouth, it has always struck me as sweet and tender. The kind of a mouth, were it a little smaller, that belongs on a woman's face. And usually is, I guess," she added with an impish grin.

Slade decided to pass that one by as unworthy of comment.

Francia was grave again. "Walt," she asked, hesitantly, "do you believe it was Sid Gholen who murdered my brother?"

"I do," he answered.

Her little hands balled into anger-trembling fists and the emerald eyes seemed to glitter.

"Careful," he warned. "Don't let your feeliings give you away. What I told you is still in strictest confidence."

"I won't," she promised, "but it won't be easy. I came close to shooting him when he hit you that first night when you were tired and worn out. Now I wish I had."

"Careful," he repeated. "You'll get more satisfaction from seeing him brought to justice in the proper and lawful way."

"I hope so," she replied morosely. "Let's forget him for the time being." She glided across to his chair.

SIXTEEN

It was one o'clock in the morning of the second day when Slade and Francia set out on their trip of exploration. They rode at but a fair pace, for Slade wished to conduct the major portion of the search by daylight. In his saddle pouches was an ample supply of provisions, plus a canteen of cold coffee and another of water. He also carried a package of ground coffee against the chance that they really would find water.

"Just like going on a picnic," Francia said.

"You won't find it exactly a picnic when we're out on the desert and the sun comes up," he warned.

Francia tossed her glowing curls. "I can take it," she declared blithely. "Don't worry about me."

"I'll admit that for a person inexperienced in desert storms, you took it pretty well the other day," he conceded. "I don't expect anything like that this trip, though. The sky's clear as a bell and there are no indications of stormy weather."

The sky *was* clear, and spangled with stars. Soon the circular edge of the late moon appeared in the east to flood the prairie with silver light. On the rangeland the night was crisply cool, with a tang of Autumn in the air. Only the steady drumming of the hoofs, the yipping of coyotes and the occasional whine of an owl broke the silence.

The horses seemed to enjoy the trip, as much as their

riders, for they snorted gaily and took playful nips at each other.

"A pity they're not male and female," observed Francia. "That would be so much nicer for them, don't you think so, dear?"

"The answer is obvious," he smiled. Francia moved her mount closer.

The miles flowed back steadily and finally they saw the wan shimmer of the desert. At its edge Slade slowed the pace.

"The going will be harder now and I want to keep the horses in good shape for the hot hours," he explained.

They were far out on the sands when the east flushed primrose and gold, and the sun rose in flaming majesty. The heat quickly increased appreciably.

"It's hot and it's lonely but it's beautiful," Francia said, gazing about wide-eyed. "I think I could quickly learn to love the desert."

"There is a fascination to it," Slade admitted. "Small wonder that men spend their lives wandering over it. Searching for gold, they say, but I think they're little interested in finding more than they need to keep them going. The desert is their home and all else seems small and crowded. Perhaps theirs is the true wisdom; I've often thought it so."

> "The wind and the stars and the lonely sands,
> As a nestling rests in the cup of His hands . . ."

she quoted softly. "Remember? Your song, the one you sang for me."

The sun rose higher and the heat increased as they forged steadily ahead. Slade searched the terrain with his eyes, estimating the distance to the sunken bowl that was his real objective. With the sun well up the slant of the eastern sky he called a halt in the shade of a tall outcropping of rock, with a straggle of mesquite close by.

"Might as well stop and make a fire and eat," he announced. "Been a long time since dinner and we're not likely to find a better place."

Francia also had canteens of water and coffee in her pouches, so neither they nor the horses lacked for drink.

"I'm starved and didn't know it," she declared as bacon and eggs sizzled in the skillet and coffee bubbled in the bucket. "This is wonderful. Didn't I tell you it would be just like a picnic?"

"This is the easy half," he warned. "Just wait till the sun is straight overhead and we're in that infernal bowl. Then you may sing another song."

"I won't," she retorted. "I'll love that, too," Slade chuckled and put more bacon in the skillet.

They ate their simple meal with the appetite of youth and perfect health. Then after a couple of cigarettes they cinched up and continued on their way.

It was far past noon when they finally reached the bowl and sent the horses down the sag. At the bottom the heat was terrific. Slade glanced anxiously at his companion. Her lips were red, her eyes wide and glowing. Yes, she could take it. Reassured, he gazed about.

"Here goes to find out," he said, and headed Shadow for the lowest of the dunes.

The slope was gentle, the sand hard packed, and the horses experienced no difficulty negotiating the slope. They reached the crest and before them was a flat expanse. Slade shook his head and turned Shadow.

"Not here," he said. "Now goes for the tallest one. I've a notion that is it, if the theory doesn't blow up in our faces."

The theory, so called, was incidentally based on a sound knowledge of geology and the vagaries of subterranean water. Slade was still fairly sanguine as to its accuracy. Nevertheless, he experienced anxiety as they climbed the slope of the big dune. Maybe he was deluding himself with too great hope.

They reached the crest and reined in. Slade uttered an exultant exclamation.

"I believe it's paydirt," he told the girl. "Sure looks that way."

Here was no profitless expanse of packed sand, but a depression in the center of the crest. It was perhaps fifty yards in diameter. They sent the horses forward to pause on the lip of the depression. Slade again exclaimed aloud. Before them was a gentle slope and at its bottom was a wide pool of water or what looked very much like it.

"Down we go," he said. "Keep your fingers crossed against it being just a mirage."

"It's no mirage!" Francia exclaimed as they reached the bottom. "Darling, that's real water or I never saw any. And look!" she exclaimed excitedly. "Hoof prints all around its edge. There have been plenty of cows here."

"And look how the bank overhangs on the far side," Slade added. "Shade for the critters during the hot hours. Where they can rest and be all set for the rest of the trip to the Rio Grande. Yes, we've found it, the hidden water known to the Indians and of which the wide-loopers somehow learned. A perfect set-up. See where fires have been kindled, a lot of them."

Slade tasted the water and found it sweet, and fairly cool. Evidently the pool was fed by springs deep down in the sands; springs that were in the nature of artesian wells, the water being forced upward by pressure caused by the subsidence which, ages before, had formed the bowl. What had created the dunes he was not certain, but thought it very likely that their core was rock which had also been forced upward in the course of the convulsion responsible for the formation. Around the core, from which doubtless the springs had spouted, the sand had drifted and been packed by the wind and the rain until they reached their present proportions.

Theory to an extent, of course, but foundationed on his knowledge of geology, and he believed it to be substantially correct. He flipped out the bits and allowed the horses to drink their fill.

Under the overhang and near where the fires had been kindled were several lanterns with oil in the bowls, a few cooking utensils, a couple of dry and moldy loaves of bread and some unopened meat tins.

"But this is no hole-up," he told the girl. "It's just a stopping point for the cows to drink and rest. I'd hoped we might find evidence of some sort of a lay-over. Their hole-up, if there is one, must be elsewhere."

"Couldn't it be Gholen's ranchhouse?" Francia suggested.

"Possibly, but somehow I don't think it is," Slade replied. "I've a notion that perhaps not all his riders are in on the deal. Some may be legitimate hands with no knowledge of his extra-curricular activities. I've run across such a thing before. But let's be trailing our twine. I wouldn't want them by some chance to catch us here; we'd be setting quail."

With the possibility in mind, he approached the crest of

the depression with caution. But the desert stretched lonely and deserted. Reassured by no signs of life they descended to the inferno of the lower bowl and rode across it as swiftly as they dared. Slade glanced at the girl. He could see the strain was telling on her a bit, but she uttered no complaint and only breathed a sigh of relief as they reached the lip of the bowl where the air seemed almost cool by contrast.

At a steady pace they crossed the desert, suffering considerable discomfort that, however, was not beyond endurance. The sun was nearing the horizon when they reached the grasslands and the Rio Grande, where Slade removed the rigs and let the horses drink and roll and graze.

"Here we follow the river north," he told the girl. "Thank Pete we brought plenty of chuck with us; we're in for another camp-out."

"Wonderful!" Francia exclaimed. "Didn't I tell you I'd enjoy every minute of it? Even down in that awful bowl, it was beautiful. The slopes are so vivid in coloring; it was like a fairyland."

"I've got a more fitting name for it, although I'll agree as to the beauty," he replied. "Hard to properly appreciate it, though, with your blood beginning to boil."

They sat by the water's edge and rested for a while, watching the river turn to flaming purple and the western hills blaze with scarlet and gold. Then they saddled up and rode north until dusk. They made camp in a thicket, cooked and ate and stowed the utensils.

"I'll admit I'm pretty well tired out," Francia said drowsily. "I think I'll stretch out on the blanket by the fire for just a minute."

Slade smiled. A moment later he chuckled softly. She was already sound asleep.

They continued riding north at daybreak, veering to the east but bypassing the desert and arriving at the ranchhouse in the late afternoon.

"First, I'll get you some coffee and then I want to shower and wash the dust out of my hair before we eat," Francia said.

She brought the coffee and vanished upstairs. Slade made himself comfortable and pondered the best use to make of what he had learned.

That the outlaws only used the pool as a watering place

and to rest the cattle during the hot hours of the day was self-evident. So any hope to lay a trap for them there was dependent on either foreknowledge of their intentions or correctly anticipating their moves. Either of which posed plenty of difficulties. If they wide-looped a herd and he learned of it in time, he'd know where to look for them. This, however, was largely based on wishful thinking. As a rule, the loss of cattle was not discovered until considerable time had elapsed.

The time-honored expedient of baiting the trap with a herd placed convenient for rustling would not work in this instance. Conditions being what they were, it would be too darned obvious, and Slade credited Gholen and the shrewd Alf Crane with enough acumen to see through such a stratagem.

Remained the possibility that the outlaws had a secret hole-up somewhere in the neighborhood. Fine! But how to locate it? That was a poser.

Well, he'd located the hidden water in the face of the contention by those who were supposed to know that there was none. So perhaps something would work out. He dismissed the problem for the time being and relaxed in comfort.

Soon the hands streamed in from the range. They greeted Francia and Slade uproariously.

"Beginning to think you two had flewed the coop," said Sime Collins.

"We just took a little ride," Slade replied lightly.

"Just around the barn and back, I reckon," Collins commented dryly. The hands chuckled and headed for the dining room. Collins lingered a moment with Slade.

"Chore's taken care of," he announced. "We ran the last bunch north this afternoon.

"Funny," he added, "but a lot of Jackson Haynes's critters have been strayin' onto our range. Maybe because our cows are gone and they figure they have a clear field. Anyhow they're coming, bunches of them." He chuckled.

"Haynes's boys will do some tall swearing when they start combing them outa the brakes and arroyos for the beef round-up. The round-up is going to be duck soup for us. Already got a darn good spot tally, and on our open north range it'll be just like herdin' 'em on a corral pasture. Yep, but Haynes's bunch will have their hands full."

Slade received this bit of news with interest. For a moment he sat in thoughtful silence, arrived at a decision.

"Sime," he said. "after dinner drop in here with me for a while. I've something to tell you, something I think you should know."

"Okay," the old rannie nodded. "I'll be here."

He was, and Slade proceeded to give him an account of what he had discovered in the course of his trip across the desert. Collins swore, astounded.

"So there really was something to what the old-timers said they heard, about the Indians running stock across the desert," he marveled. "I always thought it was so much sheep dip. So that's how the hellions do it! Well, looks like we might be able to give 'em a mite of a jar."

"Yes, if they take a notion to make another try and we learn of it in time," Slade agreed. "What you told me of Haynes's cows straying onto our range set me to thinking. There's very little chance of them doing any more pilfering from the Rocking T, now that our critters are all up to the north, but Haynes's stuff might tempt them. He has good stock."

"No better in the section," agreed Collins. "Yep, they might try to drop a loop on some of those strays that bunch around the waterholes at night. Shall we keep a watch down there?"

Slade shook his head. "Too much ground to cover," he decided. "I'll try and think up something else. Keep a tight *látigo* on your jaw, Sime; I don't want anybody aside from the three of us to know about that hidden desert water. So long as the wide-loopers don't know we know of it, we have got a chance to hit them where it'll hurt the most."

"Don't worry about me doing any talking," Collins replied.

Slade felt that there was no cause for him to do so.

Early the following morning, Slade rode west. Later in the day, Francia would ride to town. He ordered her to have Collins ride with her, so that she would have company on the night trip back to the *casa*. Francia offered no objections.

"I don't know how you do it," marveled Collins. "Used to be nobody could tell her what to do or what not to do. Now she just says, 'Yes, Walt,' and does what you say."

"She's using her head, that's all," Slade explained. "She knows that with the kind of things that have been happening hereabouts of late it isn't good for a woman to be out on the range alone at night."

"Uh-huh, I reckon that's it," Collins returned, looking not at all convinced.

SEVENTEEN

LEAVING THE RANCHHOUSE, Slade rode straight for the cliffs and the slopes and the shallow jumble of craggy hills beyond.

"What we're going to do is like looking for the proverbial needle in a haystack," he told Shadow. "But if the needle is there and you move enough hay, eventually you'll find it. I figure those hellions do have a hole-up somewhere and it is logical to believe that it is somewhere in the hills. We'll go see."

Shadow offered no objection and ambled on, apparently taking a philosophical view of the matter.

After climbing the slopes and crossing their crest, Slade entered the hills. He rode slowly, studying his surroundings. There were many trails criss-crossing the hills, most of them very old—Indian tracks beaten out by the padding of myriad moccasins in years gone by.

Others were fresher, and on a few he discovered the occasional faint traces of a horse's irons. Evidently they had once been ridden, but none recently.

He descended into canyons and gorges, searching them thoroughly. He rode ridges and benches and always he eyed the sky for the indubitable evidence of human occupancy—smoke.

But the blue vault remained stainless. No signs of life appeared other than those of the little creatures who made the hills their home. Birds gave no evidence of being disturbed. His progress south was slow and he had not covered half of the distance to where the hills petered out and the desert began when the lower edge of the sun was dipping behind the mountains. He rode back down the eastern slopes and headed for home.

103

"But we're not finished yet, horse, not by a jugful," he told his mount. "Tomorrow we'll work still farther south. I've a notion that down there is our real hunting ground. If it's there, and I believe it is, we'll find it."

The next day he repeated the performance, working farther and farther south, riding slowly, searching with even greater care, and finding nothing.

He experienced a lessening confidence as the day wore on. Beginning to look like this particular hunch wasn't a straight one, after all.

And then, with sunset a couple of hours away, his search was rewarded. Rising straight in the still and crystal-clear air was a thread of smoke. Slade studied it and concluded its origin was about two miles distant to the southwest, apparently from what appeared to be a canyon boxed on the east and with sloping sides, and only a few miles north of where the hills ended shortly before the desert began.

At the moment he was riding a bench that curved around a hill and which quite probably extended to the lip of the canyon. He carefully plotted the smoke in relation to various visible landmarks and rode on.

From time to time the blue thread would vanish, then resume again as fresh fuel was thrown on the fire which produced it.

His surmise as to the extent of the bench proved accurate. It did lead to the edge of the canyon. Below stretched the not too steep slope, sparsely grown with brush. On the lip he pulled up and eyed the descent dubiously. The smoke was no longer visible, doubtless because the fire had burned down to a bed of coals suitable for cooking. But he figured its source was still a mile or so to the west.

Just the same, however, it would be ticklish business riding down the slope, clearly outlined in the blaze of the near setting sun. If somebody was down there keeping a watch on the slope, he would be a perfect target. Nevertheless he resolved to risk it. His curiosity was at white heat. Of course he might be approaching only the campfire of some harmless prospector, but he didn't think that was the case. So far as he had heard, there was little metal in the shallow range of hills, nothing to cause a desert rat to enter them.

"Let's go, horse," he told Shadow. "If we lean against

the hot end of a slug, we'll at least know our hunch was a straight one, maybe."

With which he tackled the slope, constantly searching the terrain below with eyes that missed nothing. The floor of the narrow gorge was already shadowy, but there appeared to be no movement or other sign of life. He felt somewhat better when he passed beyond the belt of sunshine and entered the shadow of the opposite slope. Without incident he reached the canyon floor.

But it was not much better and some ways worse than the slope. It was brush grown, but the clumps of bushes were not tall enough to hide a mounted man, while they would conceal a man on foot. He was still easy prey for any lurking watcher with malevolent intentions.

The floor of the canyon was strewn with loose rock upon which Shadow's irons clicked sharply. Once he kicked one which brought up against another with a ringing bang like a thunderclap in the stillness of the coming night.

When they were still a quarter of a mile distant from where he estimated was the origin of the smoke, Slade had enough of it. He turned Shadow's nose toward the far slope, where the growth was thicker and a trifle taller. In the outer straggle he dismounted.

"Shanks' mare from here on for me, horse," he said. "The racket you're making would wake the dead. Take it easy. I'll be back shortly, I hope."

With which he stole forward through the brush, feeling much better. Now he was on more of an equal footing with anyone he might meet, although he had about arrived at the conclusion that there was nobody posted a distance from the fire. Now all he had to do was find the fire, which should be simple enough.

It wasn't. He strained his eyes to catch its glow, but the canyon, in which now the shadows were curdling, stretched on and on with no flicker of flame, no winking of sparks against the deepening dark.

Now the slope on his left had been replaced by a line of cliffs that no doubt extended to the mouth of the gorge, and the growth was becoming more and more sparse. A little farther on he halted with a mutter of exasperation.

The growth had ceased altogether and he could see ahead for hundreds of yards, the vista was absolutely barren. And

105

he was positive that he had reached the point from where the smoke had risen.

There was still enough light to make objects visible and his gaze roamed back and forth in search of some solution to the mystery. Suddenly it centered on the cliff to his left. Slanting gently up its surface was a ledge that continued until it curved around a bulge a hundred feet or so above, and vanished from his sight. It was not very broad, but broad enough to accomodate a horse and rider, and its surface appeared flat. Now to where did that thing lead, he wondered.

He was determined to find out. The ledge reached the canyon floor only a short distance from where he stood. A moment later he was creeping up it, very cautiously, and liking it not at all, for once again he was clearly visible to anyone below. He breathed a little easier when he rounded the bulge and was obscured from a portion, at least, of the canyon floor.

The ledge climbed on, the ascent still gentle. Now the crest of the cliffs was no great distance above. And to his nostrils came the unmistakable smell of wood smoke. Slowing his pace, he rounded a second bulge and halted abruptly.

The ledge had ended at an opening through a stand of brush which crowded close. The opening led to a flat space of considerable extent, with the cliffs rising above and hemming it in on all sides.

At the base of the cliffs tall brush grew thickly. And directly ahead and only a few yards distant was an old but tight-appearing cabin with one glowing window.

Slade's heart leaped exultantly. Looked like he'd found it, the outlaws' hidden hole-up. And evidently there was somebody in the cabin. His gaze traveled past the shack and centered on a leanto under which stood a single horse lacking saddle and bridle. Which seemed to indicate that there was but one person in the cabin. Now if he could just get the drop on the hellion and take him prisoner, there was a mighty good chance of acquiring valuable information, perhaps all he needed to enable him to twirl his loop. He glanced around the empty clearing and took a step forward.

His ankle slammed against something and he almost pitched headlong. Frantically he hurled himself backward, lost his balance and fell half on his side, striking the ground with stunning force, his head whacking solidly against a rock. His foot, hooked under a rope stretched across the opening, jerked convulsively.

There was a crashing roar and buckshot screeched through the space his body had occupied an instant before.

Half stunned, red flashes storming before his eyes, Slade lay motionless, blood from a cut near the edge of his forehead streaming over his face.

The flashes ceased, his vision cleared and his eyes focused on a man advancing cautiously toward him, a cocked gun in his hand. And the muzzle of the gun was trained on his prostrate form.

The fellow took a step forward, hesitated, took another step, peering with outstretched neck. Slade lay motionless, with narrowed eyes, scarcely daring to breathe. The slightest move or sign of life on his part would mean death.

Now the man was standing almost over him. He stooped, saw the blood that visored Slade's face with scarlet, and gave a grunt of satisfaction. He straightened up, holstering the gun.

Slade's hands shot out, gripped his ankles and jerked with all his strength. The fellow gave a yell of fright and fell. He managed to draw the gun as he went down but Slade's steely fingers closed on his wrist before he could bring it to bear. Instantly they were locked in a deadly struggle.

Back and back, Slade bent his opponent's gunhand, forcing the muzzle away from his own face. Powerful fingers closed on his throat with a throttling grip. He tore at the man's corded wrist but could not jerk it free. Most of his strength was devoted to forcing the gunhand back and back. His throat was closed, his lungs bursting for want of air. The red flashes were back, flickering before his eyes. His grip on the fellow's wrist slipped a little. He gave a frantic lunge as the black muzzle swung toward his head.

The gun exploded, the flame scorching Slade's cheek. The other gave a gurgling scream, the gun dropped from his nerveless hand, his legs thrashed madly. Blood gushed over Slade's hand. His antagonist had shot himself through the throat.

EIGHTEEN

GASPING FOR BREATH, Slade rolled away from the corpse. For minutes he lay breathing in hoarse gasps, trembling in every limb, his heart pounding like a muffled drum.

Gradually his strength returned, the trembling ceased, his pulses slowed to something like normal. Still sick and dizzy he sat up, holding his bloody face in his hands, retching. It was some minutes before he felt equal to standing.

Slowly he got to his feet, fumbled a handkerchief and wiped most of the blood from his face and hands. Leaning against the cliff wall, he managed to roll and light a cigarette. A few deep drags helped and soon he was feeling something like himself. Altogether, it had been as ghastly a few minutes as he had ever experienced.

First, with the aid of a couple of matches, he examined the infernal contrivance that had so nearly handed him his comeuppance. A sawed-off shotgun was wired to a stout trunk of the growth, its twin muzzles trained on the opening. The thin rope which spanned the opening was brought up under a limb and tied to the shotgun triggers, so that a jerk on the rope would fire both barrels. A man either on foot or on horseback would be almost sure to receive the double charge of buckshot. Simple but devilishly effective. Only his convulsive backward leap in an endeavor to keep from falling had saved him.

Striking another match, he peered at the dead gunman. His blood-smeared face was unfamiliar. Slade wasted little time on him for he wanted to take a look at the cabin and its contents, and he had an uneasy feeling that other members of the band might appear at any moment; he was in no condition to face a desperate fight against odds.

The door of the cabin stood open. Inside, a bracket lamp cast a ruddy glow, coals still smoldered in the fireplace, over which an iron pot simmered. Steam arose from the spout of a coffeepot. On a table was a hunk of bread.

Slade first investigated the contents of the pot. It contained pork and beans and by the size of the portion he decided the dead man had been cooking a meal for only himself. Which somewhat reassured him. Appeared the fellow had not been expecting company in the near future. El Halcón decided to risk a tin mug of coffee from the steaming pot. That helped.

Confident that the danger of immediate interruption was slight, he ladeled a portion of the hot pork and beans into a tin plate that stood on the table. That and a few nibbles of bread also helped. He purposely left the unwashed mug and plate on the table to indicate that the sojourner in the cabin had cooked and eaten a meal before riding off somewhere for reasons of his own. The body and the horse, of course, must be disposed of against the probability of others visiting the cabin, which he thought very likely.

His hunger and thirst assuaged, he examined the cabin and its contents with care. It gave every indication of having known off-and-on occupancy for a considerable length of time. There were bunks built along the walls, covered by tumbled blankets. A store of provisions rested on shelves. In a corner stood half a dozen rifles. Fuel was stacked by the fireplace, along with a bucket of fresh water.

Rummaging about on the shelves, he discovered a box nearly full of shotgun cartridges. He deftly removed the shot from two. He felt it wise to rig up the contraption which guarded the clearing. But with the shot removed from the shells, any innocent individual who might happen to prowl the ledge would get the devil scared out of him when the blanks let go, instead of having his head blown from his shoulders. Repairing to the brush-flanked opening, he replaced the spent cartridges with the blanks, cocked the gun and arranged the trip as before. He carefully wiped out the muzzles of the gun to remove all evidence that it had recently been fired. He gave the body of the slain outlaw a quick once-over and discovered nothing of importance. Next he explored the clearing.

Several large mounds of earth, now grass grown, near the far cliff wall, enclosing a circular shaft of unknown depth explained the existence of the cabin in this isolated place. Some wandering prospector, many years before, had discovered metal worth working and had thrown together the

109

roughly built shack in which he doubtless resided for an extensive period. Somehow the outlaws had hit on it and recognized it as an excellent hole-up.

Rooting about in the starlight, Slade found a sizeable boulder which he dropped down the shaft. From the sound of the rock striking bottom he concluded that the hole was quite deep and suitable for his purpose. He packed the corpse across the clearing and dropped it down the shaft.

"Guess that will hold you," was his requiem for the dead owlhoot.

Next in order was the horse. More groping about and he found the rig hanging from a peg under the leanto. He cinched it in place and led the horse, a good-looking animal with a blurred and practically uncipherable brand, to the cabin door. Entering, he made sure there was no trace of his visit that would alarm the outlaws when next they visited the shack. He blew out the lamp, closed the door and headed for the canyon floor below, leading the cayuse around the shotgun trap. At the bottom of the ledge he mounted and rode to where Shadow waited, where he changed steeds and headed toward the western mouth of the canyon, leading the outlaw's horse which would be kept under cover at the ranch.

"Well, we found it," he told Shadow. "But what to do with it now we've got it, I'm darned if I know. Hole up in the neighborhood and wait for the hellions to put in an appearance? Not so good. No way to tell if the devil we really want to drop a loop on will accompany them. Well, maybe we'll get a break of some sort or another. June along, jughead, we've got a long ride ahead of us."

It was a long ride, for he was forced to skirt the southern terminus of the hills before continuing north by east. The after effect of the excitement was setting in and he was very tired. His powder-burned cheek was sore, but not too bad. The cut on his forehead trifling.

A very lucky cut, he thought. The blood flowing from it and smearing his face had deceived the outlaw into thinking he had gotten the double charge of the shotgun. Otherwise the ending might have been quite different.

When he entered the living room of the *casa,* after caring for the horses, he found Francia asleep in a chair. She roused up instantly and stared in horror at his blood encrusted face.

"Oh, good heavens!" she gasped and ran to him. "You're hurt! What in the world happened? Where have you been?"

"Just scratches," he replied. "I'll tell you all about it later. Got some coffee handy?"

She flew to the kitchen to prepare coffee and food. Slade went to the bathroom and enjoyed a good wash, after which he felt much better.

With the coffee and the food on the table between them, Slade told her everything, slurring over his desperate battle with the outlaw.

Francia wasn't fooled. She shuddered convulsively. "I don't see how you've managed to stay alive as long as you have," she declared. "It would appear your life is dedicated to violence."

"I don't look for it," he protested, "and anyhow I always seem to muddle through. Wyatt Earp and Bill Tilghman, for instance, went through a lot more than I have—" which was just about true— "and they're still alive and kicking."

"Yes, I suppose Providence keeps watch over you because you have work in the world to do," she said. "But you're darned hard on the nerves. What's your next move?"

"I don't know," he admitted frankly. "Just wait and see which way the cat jumps, I suppose."

Which was just about how the situation stood. He believed the outlaws would cut loose somewhere before long and perhaps provide him with opportunity. Cattle stealing was big business in Texas and the dealers in wide-looped beef were as insistent on steady and prompt delivery as were the legitimate buyers. Besides, an outlaw leader had to keep his men supplied with money if he hoped to hold them in check. Otherwise they were liable to strike out on their own and perhaps bring disaster for all concerned.

So, everything considered, he felt fairly sanguine toward the future.

"And now it's time you went to bed," Francia told him. "There's a limit to what even you can endure. Next thing you know you'll end up with a sick spell. Don't argue with me, now, I know where you belong."

"Yes, dear," he replied meekly, and did as she said.

111

NINETEEN

WHEN SLADE AWAKENED, the sun was shining brilliantly in a clear sky. He moved a little and discovered quite a few sore spots and some stiffness. His scorched cheek was also sore, but not unduly so.

"Guess that big hellion left me something to remember him by," he yawned. "Well, it'll soon wear off."

Before getting up he lay for a while reviewing recent events and pondering his next move. He wondered if it would be wise to keep a watch on Gholen's ranchhouse and try to trail the side-winder. After due consideration he concluded the notion was not a good one. In the first place, Gholen's ranchhouse sat on the open prairie with a clear view in every direction, with no cover anywhere close. Also, he could hardly keep watch twenty-four hours a day, and there was no telling when the ranch owner might take a notion to head for somewhere. Looked like, as he told Francia, he'd just have to wait and see which way the cat would jump.

He got up, bathed and shaved and descended to the living room, where Francia awaited him; she wore her riding costume.

"After you've had your breakfast I'm heading for town and a last talk with Burk," she explained. "Like to ride with me?"

"Don't see any reason why I shouldn't," he agreed. "Nothing to do here that Collins can't take care of."

His breakfast finished and a cigarette smoked, Slade got the rigs on Shadow and her big bay and they set out. It was a beautiful day and they rode mostly in silence, for the sheer loveliness of the range seemed to forbid speech. When they reached the saloon, Francia and Burk went into conference. Slade repaired to the kitchen for a palaver with Stiffy.

"Your *amigo* Gholen was in here a little while ago," the cook announced. "Seemed peeved as a teased snake about something. I've a notion he's sorta put out over Francia selling out to Burk. He's sorta figured himself a privileged character hereabouts, I reckon, but that won't go with Burk. He holds his comb rather high and don't cowtow to anybody. A cold proposition, too, if you get him riled. Gholen won't get anywhere with Burk."

"Was Crane with him?" Slade asked. Stiffy shook his head.

"Nope, but another jigger was. Sort of an important-looking jigger with blue jowls and eyes that seemed to be looking everywhere at once. Wonder who he was?"

Slade had a strong notion that he was very likely a dealer in stolen cattle but refrained from saying so, for he was not sure. The supposition rendered him thoughtful.

"You staying on with Burk?" he asked by way of making conversation. Stiffy again shook his head.

"Nope," he replied. "I'm moving out to the ranch. Francia wants me to and I can still do a chore of riding. Miguel will take over the kitchen; he's a good cook and Burk likes him."

"I've a notion Burk will make out," Slade commented. The old cook nodded agreement.

Stiffy went about his various chores. Slade sat smoking and thinking. He was interested in Stiffy's remarks anent Sid Gholen's companion. If the fellow really was a dealer in wet cows, he might well have come to urge Gholen to get busy and supply him with something with which to meet his commitments. So far as Slade knew there had been no wide-looping in the section since the abortive attempt to run off Jackson Haynes's herd, which he, Slade, had frustrated. Quite likely the boys on the far side of the Rio Grande were getting hungry.

Slade and Francia remained at the saloon until late. Sid Gholen did not reappear.

Before leaving, Slade paused at the kitchen to say good-night to Stiffy. The old cook chuckled and wagged his gray head.

"Feller, you've sure raised heck and shoved a chunk under a corner since you coiled your twine here," he said. "Wide-loopers thinned out, the saloon business changed hands. And Francia! No more a hellcat. Just another nice woman doing what a man tells her to do. How in blazes did you work it?"

Slade laughed, refrained from explaining and went in quest of Francia. They rode home under the stars.

"What are you thinking about, dear?" she asked as they

neared the ranchhouse. "You've hardly spoken a word all the way. I believe you've forgotten all about me."

"Impossible!" he replied. "Easier to forget the stars and the sunshine."

"That was sweet," she laughed, "but just what *were* you thinking?"

"I was wondering," he said, "just when and in which way the cat will jump."

However, to Slade's disgust, the cat remained inactive. All was peace on the rangeland. Plans were being made for the beef round-up, now not far off. Wide-loopers were conspicuous in their absence.

"But it won't last," he told Shadow. "the hellions will bust loose someplace and soon. Watch what I tell you."

Shadow refrained from comment and stretched his legs.

Francia and Slade rode to town and sat as customers in Burk's place, and enjoyed the novelty of the experience.

"Every now and then I see something that makes me want to jump up and correct it," she confided. "Then I remember it's none of my business, and I'm glad of it."

"Don't you miss your whip?" he teased.

"I never want to see or touch another whip," she declared. "Unless it would be to wear one out on the mule skinner who taught me how to use it."

And then, a few days later, the cat did jump, and in the direction Slade hoped it would. Shortly before mid morning one of Jackson Haynes's punchers rode up to the *casa* in a very bad temper.

"You fellers aren't to blame, of course," he said, as he accepted coffee and a snack, "but you've sure caused us trouble. When you ran your cows north, our critters figured they might as well take over, and they've been doing just that. Well, last night we lost nigh onto a hundred head from around a waterhole down there."

Without delay, Slade hurried to the bunkhouse, where Sime Collins and a half dozen of the hands, their morning chores finished and with nothing more to do, were whiling away the time at poker. He repeated what the J Bar H puncher said.

"I'm riding," he announced. "Is there anybody here who doesn't mind taking a chance and would like to ride with me?"

The next moment cards and chips were scattered over the

floor and all seven were on the run to the corral pasture and their horses.

Slade returned to the house and told Francia what he had in mind. Her face whitened, but she did not attempt to dissuade him.

"All right," she said, "I'll be waiting for you."

"I figure it's showdown," he said. "After which we'll have a little peace and quiet hereabouts for a change."

"I hope so," she replied despondently. "I hope so. Please take care of yourself."

The Haynes puncher set down his coffee cup in a hurry. "And I'm going along, if you'll let me," he said.

"Glad to have you," Slade answered. "Let's go."

A few minutes later Francia, one hand pressed to her mouth, watched them ride away south by west across the prairie. She turned back to the house, her lips moving in prayer.

As they rode, Slade recounted his experiences on the desert and his discovery of the hidden water. Sime Collins smiled, but the others burst into astonished exclamations.

"My granddad once told me about his dad knowing Indians who knew about that water," one remarked. "I didn't pay it much mind, figuring it was just talk, but I reckon it wasn't."

"It's not such an unusual formation," Slade said. "I've heard of others, and I once saw one somewhat similar. The big chore was finding it."

"Uh-huh, a chore nobody else has been able to finagle in the past hundred years or so," Sime Collins observed dryly. "Feller, you're a wonder!"

The others nodded sober agreement.

Once they were well away from the ranchhouse, Slade curbed his companions' eagerness and slowed the pace.

"We've got a long ride ahead of us and the major portion across the desert," he explained. "We want to keep our horses in the best possible shape. That's an advantage the hellions will enjoy; their cayuses will be fresh after a day of rest and plenty of water. If they get the jump on us and skalley-hoot, we'll never catch them up."

Each man packed canteens of water in his saddle pouches, chiefly for the benefit of his mount, and Slade felt that the horses would not suffer too severely from thirst. But the heat would be enervating to man and beast, and if a wind kicked up the dust, the going would be hard indeed. However, he hoped for the best and rode in a fairly equable frame of mind.

As they rode across the sparkling rangeland, the cowboys chattered gaily, but once out on the desert they soon fell silent. The heat was bad, worse than Slade had experienced in the course of his other trips, and there was enough wind to stir the sands and raise considerable dust.

He gleaned a grain of comfort from that, however; it would render them less liable to detection as they approached the bowl, which they must reach before full dark were they to surprise the outlaws in its depths, which he earnestly desired to do. For with the descent of the cool of night, they would start the cows moving and did they reach the open desert, the advantage would be theirs.

Soon the horses' gait slowed to a walk, a shamble. Shadow alone did not appear greatly affected and seemed to regard his fellow cayuses' distress with contempt. He was an excellent desert horse and experienced in such wastelands. Nor did his rider show any noticeable signs of discomfort.

"Keep your neckerchief over your nose and mouth," he cautioned. "Breathe slow and breathe deep, and relax. We'll make it."

The others mumbled confident agreement and followed his advice.

The slow miles slogged past. The sun slid down the western slant of the sky. Slid too swiftly for Slade's peace of mind. He felt sure that his sense of distance and direction would not play him false, nevertheless, he experienced a growing disquietude. It seemed to him that they had already covered the necessary quota of miles. He anxiously scanned the terrain ahead. The wind had lost some force and the air was clearer.

The lower edge of the sun was touching the horizon when, with a sigh of relief, he recognized the long slope that led to the rim of the bowl.

They breasted the sag, tense and eager, slowing the horses more and more. Three fourths of the way up was a scattering of thicket. When they reached it, Slade called a halt.

"Here we'll leave the horses," he said. "They'll stand—they're too tired to move without urging."

For a long moment he scanned the lip of the bowl, outlined against the sunset sky. There was no one in sight. He had felt fairly confident that the outlaws, not fearing pursuit, would be unlikely to post a sentry outside the depression and was thankful to see that his surmise had been correct.

"Down on your hands and knees and crawl the rest of the way," he ordered, setting the example. Keeping a little to the front, he reached the rim of the bowl first and motioned the others to halt. Cautiously he peered over the lip. Below lay the floor of the bowl, devoid of signs of life, and he could hear no sound. He wondered uneasily if he had been outwitted, if the wide-loopers, abandoning their usual practice, had run the cows north to New Mexico. For long minutes he peered and listened, while his companions crouched expectantly behind him.

Still no sound, no movement as he contemplated beginning the descent. Then from the crest of the highest dune, which loomed well above the rim of the bowl, a spiral of smoke appeared, barely visible against the darkening sky. He uttered an exultant exclamation and turned to the others.

"They're there," he whispered. "Looks like they're cooking something to eat. Let's go, and for Pete's sake, be quiet."

Creeping down the far sag was an unpleasant chore. Should someone appear on the crest of the dune they would almost certainly be spotted.

It was even worse on the level expanse of the bowl bottom, where the slowly dying light seemed to concentrate. Slade slowed the pace until they progressed at barely a crawl, for a stationary object might be passed over, while movement would be more open to detection.

Scarcely daring to breathe, they crept on, pausing at times to listen and scan the crest of the dune that stood out hard and clear against the still-glowing sky. The relief of tension was almost physically painful when at last they reached the dune and flattened against its side. Slade studied his surroundings, turned to his followers.

"Right over there around the bulge is where I figure they'll come down—it's the logical route," he whispered. "The cows will come first and the riders will be bunched behind them, which will be all to the good. We'll wait till they're almost to the bottom. Hold everything till I give the word, then follow my lead. We are acting as law abiding peace officers and must give them a chance to surrender, which I don't think they'll do. When the ball opens, shoot fast and shoot straight. Everything understood?"

The others nodded and settled themselves to wait.

TWENTY

IT WAS A RATHER LONG WAIT and a tedious one. The sky was losing its flame of color, for the sun was well down with only reflected light still pouring up from behind the western crags, seeming to focus on the depths of the bowl.

And then from above came a sound, the querulous bleat of a disturbed steer.

"They're coming," Slade breathed. "Get set." He drew both guns and peered around the shallow bulge.

From above came more sounds, a scrambling of hoofs as the cows toiled up the inner slope of the depression, the shouts of men, a clicking of bridle irons. In contrast to the prevailing hush of a moment before, the racket was startlingly loud.

Now the scuttering of hoofs and the querulous grumbling drew steadily nearer; the cattle were coming down the outer slope of the dune. The sharper click of horses' irons could be distinguished. The posse tensed for action.

On the slope a little to the right abruptly loomed the lead cows, stumbling and sliding. They streamed onto the level ground, snorting and complaining. And close on the heels of the last stragglers bulged a tight group of mounted men. Slade counted eight altogether. In the forefront was the tall form of Sid Gholen, with Alf Crane, his range boss, slouching in his saddle beside him. Slade's voice rang out, thundering above the thudding of the cattle's hoofs, "Elevate! You're covered!"

There was an instant of utter silence, then a bellow of

118

curses. As he saw, in the uncertain half-light, the gleam of shifted metal, Slade shot with both hands—trying to line sights with Gholen—who had crowded in behind one of his men.

The cowboys joined in, whooping and yelling and firing as fast as they could pull trigger. Three saddles were emptied by that first booming volley. A fourth man went down, kicking and yelling as Slade shot left and right.

Taken utterly by surprise, demoralized, the remaining outlaws nevertheless fought back viciously. A cowboy beside Slade yelped with pain as a slug ripped his arm. Another gave a queer, choking grunt and pitched forward on his face.

Now the wide-loopers were down on the level and tangled up with the milling cattle, providing uncertain targets.

"Got another one!" whooped Collins. Another instant and a sixth saddle was empty.

Through the milling herd tore two horsemen, going like the wind, knocking the cows right and left with their charging horses.

"It's Gholen and Alf Crane!" bawled Collins. "They're getting away!"

He emptied his gun after the fugitives, with no results. Slade frantically shoved fresh cartridges into his Colt, raised it and took deliberate aim as the pair went speeding up the far slope of the bowl, practically out of sixgun range. Flame spouted from the muzzle of the six again and again. He thought he saw Alf Crane lurch, but the range boss stayed in the hull. Another moment and the fugitives reached the rim of the bowl, seemed to hesitate, then circled north and out of sight.

Collins was spouting a flood of profanity. "The ones we wanted most and they got away!" he raved in bitter disappointment.

"Never mind," Slade told him. "I'm pretty sure I know where they're headed for; I'll be after them."

"I'll go with you," Collins instantly volunteered. Slade shook his head.

"Your cayuse wouldn't be up to the twenty-five miles and better he'd have to cover before daylight," he replied. "Shadow is the only horse that can take it. Easy, now, and let's see what we bagged. "I've either got plenty of time or none at all, according to whether my hunch is a straight one or not. Any of our bunch badly hurt?"

"A couple of nicks and one creased head," a cowboy reported. "Nobody cashed in."

The others had been examining the slain owlhoots by the aid of matches.

"Here's one still kicking!" a hand whooped. "Got it through the arm. Hey, he's got the other arm tied up. Got one someplace else, I reckon."

Slade strode forward, struck a match and gazed at the cursing, moaning outlaw.

"Well! well!" he exclaimed. "Old Slow Baker himself. Picked up another little souvenir, eh?"

Baker snarled up at him like a cornered rat. Slade cut away his shirt sleeve, tore it into strips and deftly padded and bound the wounded arm to stanch the bleeding. He turned to the hands.

"In that hole on top of the dune I think you'll find some lanterns," he said. "Bring down a couple, and get the fire going again. You may find something to eat up there, too, if the hellions happened to leave any. Somebody else go get the horses and take them up to drink."

The punchers hurried to care for the chores. Slade turned back to Baker.

"I don't think you'll wriggle out of the loop this time, Slow," he said. "Now I'm giving you your choice—talk, or stretch rope; we're in no mood to fool with you."

Baker cringed away from the threat in the Ranger's cold eyes. His soul shriveled by the fear of death, he talked readily enough.

"We met Gholen over in Arizona and took up with him 'cause he was smart. He knew how to open safes, and lots of things. We did all right in Arizona, but things began to get sorta hot there so Gholen decided to come over here. He bought the spread to make it look like he was just another cowman. He knew all about this section—was brought up close to here, just over the New Mexico line. His Dad was a trapper and hunter. Educated feller, I gather, and taught Sid a lot of book learnin'. They prowled all this section for years when Sid was a kid. The old man told Sid about the Indians running cows across the desert. Sid nosed about out on the

desert and found the water here and figured how to use it
to run cows across while everybody was thinking they were
run to New Mexico. Yes, we took a sashay over east a
while back and did okay. Me and Shotgun Blue had ambled
off for a while on some business—we were brought up in this
section, too. Sid sent for us to get rid of you for him. He
figured you aimed to horn in. Reckon he was right. Yes,
he killed Tom Renshaw and robbed his safe. Killed Bates,
the Rocking T range boss, too. Bates run onto us slick-ironing
a calf. Sid wanted that fool girl, Francia, and her spread.
I figure he made a mistake there; get mixed up with a woman
and you're in for trouble. But just the same he's smart.

"Smart enough to give you the slip tonight," he added
maliciously.

"Perhaps," Slade replied. "And I suppose his father
showed him that old cabin up top the cliffs in the canyon?"

Baker stared. "Blast you, you know about that, too?"

"Yes, I know about it," Slade answered grimly. "Gholen's
headed for it, isn't he?" Baker was silent. Slade turned to
Collins, an interested listener.

"Here come the horses, Sime," he said. "Guess you might
as well get your rope. Looks like we'll have use for it."

"Fine!" exclaimed Collins, and turned to go.

"Wait! wait!" screeched Baker. "Yes, that's where he's
headed for. He figures to be safe there till he's ready to
pull out of the section. Got some *dinero* stashed away there,
I think."

"Ah, heck! why'd he have to talk?" said Collins fin-
gering his twine and looking disappointed. Slade repressed
a grin.

"Okay, Baker," he said. "You can tell the rest of the story
to the sheriff."

Before sending Shadow up the dune to drink with the
other horses, Slade secured his medicants from the saddle
pouch and cared for the wounded cowboys, whose injuries
were really quite slight.

The punchers had found, in addition to the lanterns, quite
a bit of uneaten food, so everybody had a snack. Slade even
managed to scrape up a few handfuls of oats for Shadow.

"Now I'm riding," he told Collins. "Take Slow and the
bodies to town after you've rested your broncs and turn them

121

over to the marshal. He'll notify Sheriff Harty. I see Baker's horse and the others didn't leave the bowl, so you won't lack for transportation facilities. I'll see you at the ranchhouse."

"I hope," Collins returned morosely. "I sure wish you'd let me go with you." Slade shook his head.

"I've got to reach that cabin before daylight," he replied. "I gather from what Slow said that Gholen is liable to pull out at any moment. Without him and Crane, the chore is only half done. Don't worry about me, I'll be okay."

"I don't doubt it, you always come through," Collins conceded. "Good hunting!"

With Shadow fed and watered and with nearly two hours of rest, Slade had no fear but that he would make it to the canyon before daylight. His only anxiety was that Gholen and Crane would grab the money Baker believed they had stashed in the cabin and hightail without delay. However, believing they were not subject to pursuit by the posse on jaded horses, they would more likely, he thought, hole up in their refuge for a while and then endeavor to slip out of the section under cover of darkness. If they tarried at the cabin just long enough to pick up the cash, they would be forced to make a try for New Mexico or Mexico during the daylight hours when they would be much more liable to detection. So he rode on at a fair pace, not pushing the horse. He believed he would not be very far behind his quarry when he reached the cabin in the canyon.

The night was clear, the stars brilliant. There was no wind and the temperature had dropped many degrees since nightfall. At times he felt almost cold, which was characteristic of the desert. The thermometer always fell rapidly once the sun was down, which was the case in many such wastelands; men had been known to freeze in Death Valley after a day of exhaustion because of the enervating heat.

Mile after mile flowed back under Shadow's hoofs. The great clock in the sky turned and Slade estimated it still lacked several hours till dawn when he reached the mouth of the canyon.

Now he slowed his mount and rode cautiously, constantly scanning the terrain ahead. He had no desire to suddenly run into the unsavory pair with no advance warning. He did not underestimate either Gholen or Alf Crane. Both had the reputation of being deadly with a gun, and they were desperate men with the slim shadow of the noose before their eyes.

Without incident, he approached the point where the ledge reached the canyon floor. Nowhere was there sign or sound of life. He rode on till he reached the stand of brush which would provide Shadow with concealment. With a word to the black horse, he dismounted and stole back on foot to where the ledge began. After a pause to listen, he cautiously climbed its gentle slant.

Nothing happened and he reached the brush-flanked opening. Locating the rope that stretched across the ground, to trip the shotgun trap, he stepped over it and gazed across the star-burned clearing. The solid bulk of the peak-roofed cabin loomed before him, and the window glowed golden. The quarry was undoubtedly inside. Keeping in the shadow, he edged around to the corner of the building, crept stealthily to the window and peered around the edge of the frame.

Seated at the table, smoking and talking and drinking coffee, were Sid Gholen and Alf Crane. On the table were two heaps of gold coin. A floor board ripped loose and cast aside showed where the money had been cached. Looked like the hellions were going to pull out before very long. Those heaps represented quite a sum of money. But what was more important than the money or their apparent intentions was the fact that the two men sat facing the door.

Slade studied the situation; it was not satisfactory. The only entrance to the cabin was by way of the door, which he must crash open with his shoulder. And with the two men sitting facing it, the risk was altogether too great. Somehow he must get their attention focused on the rear of the cabin for a moment, but how? Nor would it do good to wait until they stood up and started moving around. Then they would be separated and he might well find himself caught in a deadly crossfire.

For crawling moments he considered the matter with an earnestness that almost amounted to mental agony, racking his brains for a solution of the problem, which refused to come.

Then suddenly he recalled a trick he had once played under somewhat similar, but much less hazardous, conditions.

"If that darn rope is just long enough," he murmured. He

123

slid away from the window and, keeping well in the shadow, hurried back to the opening in the brush. After lowering the hammers of the shotgun, he removed the cord from the triggers and followed the rope across the opening to where it was secured on the far side. Yes, it was long enough. He groped about, discovered a sizeable boulder and secured it to one end of the cord. Then he slipped back to the window and glanced in. Gholen and Crane still sat in the same position. He ducked under the window and glided to the front of the cabin, close to the door. Holding onto one end of the rope, he pitched the boulder over the comb of the roof.

It cleared the far eaves and as the rope tightened, banged against the rear of the cabin, and again and again as Slade jerked the rope, a very creditable imitation of somebody pounding on the back wall.

In the cabin a chair overturned with a clatter. There was a volley of exclamations, a thumping of boots on the floor. Slade leaped forward, hit the door with his shoulder. It flew open and he was in the room. The two men, who were standing and staring at the rear wall, whirled around, hands streaking to their guns.

Slade drew and shot Gholen twice before his gun cleared leather. Crane's bullet slashed a red furrow across the skin of his neck as he slewed sideways and nearly knocked him off his feet with the shock. Weaving, ducking, he answered the range boss' fire, shot for shot. A moment later he lowered his Colts, and cautiously approached the two forms sprawled on the floor amid gold pieces scattered from the overturned table.

Alf Crane was dead, a blue hole between his staring eyes. Gholen, shot twice through the chest, was going fast. He glared up with hate-filled eyes as Slade bent over him.

"Blast you! why did you have to come here?" he gasped. "Why couldn't you work out your own pickings? Why did you come here?"

Slade held the star of the Rangers before the dying man's eyes.

"This is why, Gholen," he said quietly.

Sid Gholen's glazing eyes fixed on the symbol of law and order. He strove to speak again, but choked on the blood in his throat and, choking, died.

Wearily, Slade holstered his gun and righted the table. There was coffee steaming on the coals of the fire. He poured a cup and sat down, drinking it in sips. Rolling a cigarette with fingers that fumbled a little, he took several deep drags, which helped. After it was finished he rolled another, which he smoked slowly. Then he summoned enough strength to gather up the scattered money and store it in a canvas sack that lay nearby.

He did not feel like touching the bodies. Leave them, and the one down the mine shaft, as they were, intact, for the sheriff to look over and dispose of as he saw fit. Blowing out the light, he left the cabin, closing the door behind him.

Under the leanto were a couple of horses, untethered, the rigs removed, munching oats. He'd leave them for the sheriff to look after, too. He never wanted to see the ill-omened clearing again.

Stumbling down the ledge, he regained Shadow and rode out of the canyon. The dawn was flushing the eastern sky as he skirted the hills and turned north.

Francia was standing on the porch, gazing south, when he reached the ranchhouse. She ran to him as he dismounted.

"Are you all right?" she cried. "There's blood on your neck!"

"Fine as frog's hair, only a mite tired," he smiled.

She shrilled a call for a wrangler, who came running to care for Shadow.

"Bring my pouches to the house," Slade directed. Francia led him up the steps and forced him into a chair, her eyes anxious.

"You look terribly worn out," she said. "I'll fix you something to eat and then you're going to bed before you topple over."

As he ate, he recounted the happenings of the past twenty-four hours, and very nearly went to sleep over his meal. She flung an arm around his waist to support him as he shambled up the stairs.

Slade slept until nearly dusk and awoke feeling his normal self again. When he descended to the living room he found

125

Sime Collins with Francia. The old waddie looked tired but otherwise okay.

"So you made out, eh?" he chuckled. "Figured you would. Yep, we turned Baker and the carcasses over to the marshal and he sent a wire to the sheriff. Reckon he's there by now. A plumb clean-up chore, all right. Guess we won't have any more trouble hereabouts for a while."

"Come on and eat, both of you," Francia urged. "Then you can talk."

When they returned to the living room, Slade took the canvas sack from his saddle pouch and upended it on the table. Francia and Collins stared, astonished, at the flood of gold

"Better than two thousand dollars there, I figure," Slade said, and told them where he got it.

"I'd suggest that you keep half of it to part pay for the cows you lost," he said to Francia. "Divide the rest among the boys—they earned it, and it'll give them a nice bust in town. Be sure Clark, the J Bar H hand, gets his divvy.

"And you don't have to bother your head about the mortgage on the spread any more," he added. "It's not worth the paper it's written on, now. Same goes for the five thousand you thought you owed Sid Gholen. That's cleared up, too. So you're not doing so bad."

"Not financially," she agreed, with a sigh.

Sheriff Harty, accompanied by a deputy, arrived at the ranchhouse the following morning.

"So everything's taken care of, eh?" he said as he shook hands with Slade. "I'm not surprised. Let's hear about it."

Slade repeated his account of the happenings in the cabin. He added instructions how to locate the canyon in which the shack stood.

"I'll gather up the varmints," Harty said. "The coroner is at Olton and wants to hold an inquest tomorrow. You'll be there?"

"Yes, I'll be there," Slade promised.

After the sheriff and the deputy departed, he stood on the veranda, gazing south toward the unseen mountains of Mexico, his eyes brooding. He turned at Francia's touch on his arm.

"I suppose you'll be riding after the inquest?" she asked, the green eyes wistful. Slade smiled down at her.

"I'll stick around for a few days longer and rest up," he replied. "Then I'll have to be riding; I have a chore to do. I'll be riding back this way, but first I must take care of the chore. It's unfinished business."

THE END